HELP FROM THE HEART

Barbara Cartland

Barbara Cartland Ebooks Ltd

This edition © 2023

ISBNs

9781788676663   EPUB

9781788676670   PAPERBACK

Book design by M-Y Books

m-ybooks.co.uk

THE BARBARA CARTLAND ETERNAL COLLECTION

The Barbara Cartland Eternal Collection is the unique opportunity to collect all five hundred of the timeless beautiful romantic novels written by the world's most celebrated and enduring romantic author.

Named the Eternal Collection because Barbara's inspiring stories of pure love, just the same as love itself, the books will be published on the internet at the rate of four titles per month until all five hundred are available.

The Eternal Collection, classic pure romance available worldwide for all time .

THE LATE DAME BARBARA CARTLAND

Barbara Cartland, who sadly died in May 2000 at the grand age of ninety eight, remains one of the world's most famous romantic novelists. With worldwide sales of over one billion, her outstanding 723 books have been translated into thirty six different languages, to be enjoyed by readers of romance globally.

Writing her first book 'Jigsaw' at the age of 21, Barbara became an immediate bestseller. Building upon this initial success, she wrote continuously throughout her life, producing bestsellers for an astonishing 76 years. In addition to Barbara Cartland's legion of fans in the UK and across Europe, her books have always been immensely popular in the USA. In 1976 she achieved the unprecedented feat of having books at numbers 1 & 2 in the prestigious B. Dalton Bookseller bestsellers list.

Although she is often referred to as the 'Queen of Romance', Barbara Cartland also wrote several historical biographies, six autobiographies and numerous theatrical plays as well as books on life, love, health and cookery. Becoming one of Britain's most popular media personalities and dressed in her trademark pink, Barbara spoke on radio and television about social and political issues, as well as making many public appearances.

In 1991 she became a Dame of the Order of the British Empire for her contribution to literature and her work for humanitarian and charitable causes.

Known for her glamour, style, and vitality Barbara Cartland became a legend in her own lifetime. Best remembered for her wonderful romantic novels and loved by millions of readers worldwide, her books remain treasured for their heroic heroes, plucky heroines and traditional values. But above all, it was Barbara Cartland's overriding belief in the positive power of love to help, heal and improve the quality of life for everyone that made her truly unique.

AUTHOR'S NOTE

It is true that the Prince of Wales, later King Edward VII, had a special way of finding the bedrooms of beautiful women who attracted him.

As the houses where His Royal Highness stayed were usually very large, he suggested that a rose placed outside the bedroom door would simplify his search and then prevent him from making embarrassing mistakes.

The Prince married the beautiful Alexandra of Denmark in 1863, but just five years later, when their third child, Princess Victoria, was born, his love affairs were already delighting the gossips.

There were tales of enticing beauties in Russia, where the Prince attended the Wedding of Princess Alexandra's sister, Dagmar, to the Czarevitch Alexander and of many seductive Princesses and actresses in Paris, which he visited alone the following year.

There the Prince led the way and inevitably the younger members of Society followed.

To some it was a very welcome rebellion from the solemnity and the worthy preciseness of the Prince Consort and, after his early death, the gloom and boredom of Queen Victoria's unceasing mourning at Windsor Castle.

CHAPTER ONE
1870

Dinner was finished and the ladies moved into the large salon with its crystal chandeliers and masses of exotic flowers.

They looked like beautiful swans with their gowns swept back into the new bustle, which on Frederick Worth's instructions, had just supplanted the crinoline.

The bustle accentuated their tiny waists and above it tight bodices outlined their curved breasts and seemed to draw the eye to the low *décolletage*, which again had just come into vogue.

An uninformed observer might well have been surprised at the sight of so many beautiful women congregated in one room if he had not known that their host was Prince János Kovác.

Everything in Alchester Castle seemed to have surrounding it an aura of wealth that was inescapable.

Only one or two of the older members of the large house party assembled there for the weekend could remember what The Castle had looked like before the Duke of Alchester had sold it to the Prince.

"One consolation," said one Dowager glittering with a fortune in diamonds as she looked at the paintings hanging in the salon, "is that the Alchesters have not only been able to pay their bills but can now live in comparative comfort since they gave up The Castle."

"My dear, can you remember what it was like?" her companion exclaimed.

"Bitterly cold in winter and the walls and ceilings damp because the roof leaked. Nothing has been repaired or mended for at least fifty years. And the food was quite inedible!"

The Dowager laughed.

"Rather different from tonight."

There was silence as both of them thought how superb the dinner had been and how as course succeeded course the wines accompanying them had all been the joy of every epicure present.

It was inevitable that everybody should extol the Prince's possessions until they ran out of adjectives.

Prince János Kovác, who reigned over thousands of acres in the East of Hungary, had come to England in the first place to hunt.

He had been so delighted with the sport he had enjoyed in the Shires that he had not only joined several famous packs but had also set up a Racing Stable, which had already begun to win the Classics one by one.

Had he been any other young man, he would have aroused the envy and hatred of those he competed with.

But Prince János was exceedingly popular not just with those who backed his horses and then cheered him past the Winning Post, but with the Jockey Club, of which he was now a member.

Those he entertained with lavishness and generosity acclaimed him as a true sportsman after every Englishman's heart.

That invitations to his superb house parties were sought after went without saying and he contrived, someone said a little enviously, to pack more beauties into the square yard than any other host had ever managed to do.

Looking round the room at the ladies, whether they were blonde, brunette or red-headed, no one could doubt that if Paris himself had been present, he would have found it very hard to decide who he should award the Golden Apple to.

All the famous beauties of the time were known to the Prince and there was little doubt that they were fascinated, intrigued and often infatuated with him.

But strangely enough, even the most inquisitive gossipmongers of the Social world could find little to say about Prince János which was the least scandalous or even indiscreet.

However, that did not apply to his guests and, as Lady Esme Meldrum moved across the room to look at her reflection in one of the gold-framed mirrors, the Marchioness of Claydon followed her progress with hatred in her dark eyes.

There was no doubt that Lady Esme was exceedingly beautiful in the traditional mould that was accepted by all the artists of the time.

With her golden hair, her eyes the colour of a thrush's egg and a pink-and-white skin like transparent porcelain, it was impossible to think that anyone could be lovelier.

She carried herself superbly and her figure was like that of a young Goddess.

She had been married when she was eighteen to Sir Richard Meldrum, with whom she had fallen head-over-heels in love.

Her parents had expected her to make a much better match, but, as Richard Meldrum was already spoken of as one of the most promising Ambassadors in Europe, they became more reconciled to their daughter's choice.

However, after eight years of marriage to a husband who was increasingly occupied by his duties, Lady Esme was looking round for amusement.

It was fortunate for her that the Earl of Sherburn should recognise her attractions just at the moment when she had decided that he was without exception the most attractive man she had seen since she fell in love so many years ago with her husband.

Osmond Sherburn was rich, handsome, slightly bored with his success and extremely elusive when it came to the question of matrimony.

A large number of ambitious Mamas had thought that their daughters would grace the Sherburn jewels and make a very charming Chatelaine in the Earl's ancestral home and in the other houses he possessed.

But then he was wise enough to devote his attention to married women with complacent husbands. He certainly annoyed a large number of them to the point where they longed to call him out for a duel.

But the Earl's friendship with the Prince of Wales and his position in Society made them think twice and decide that to challenge him would be an undoubted mistake.

The Earl therefore enjoyed himself as he wished and he found that few women, if any, refused what he desired.

He had just had a brief but enjoyable *affaire de coeur* with the Marchioness of Claydon.

As was usual, he had begun to cool off first and he was in fact wondering how he could extricate himself from the clinging and very possessive arms of the Marchioness when Lady Esme came into view.

To say that he was bowled over would be an exaggeration for the Earl always kept his feet very firmly on the ground.

His most ardent and tempestuous love affairs were conducted with a certain amount of discretion on his part, which meant that his head always ruled his heart.

It was perhaps this more than anything else which made the women who fell in love with him aware that he was never completely their captive.

However 'siren-like' they might be and however alluring and attractive, they could not hold him forever.

"I cannot think why I lost Osmond," one beauty had sobbed to the Marchioness before she and the Earl had really become aware of each other.

"Perhaps, dear, you were too subservient," Kathie Claydon had replied.

"How can you be anything else with Osmond?" the beauty had then asked. "He is so dominating, so masterful and, because one is so thrilled by his supremacy, it is impossible to do anything but what he wishes."

The Marchioness had thought privately that from what she had seen of the Earl, she was sure that he needed a challenge.

When they next met at a house party, at which neither of them was particularly interested in anybody else, she had looked at him with Sphinx-like eyes.

She had been deliberately provocative and at the same time intriguing, inviting and very mysterious and, as she had hoped, he had responded by being ardent and possessive.

But she had found that, after the Earl had become her lover, her willpower had gone and she could no longer challenge him as she had intended.

Instead she became entirely submissive and obedient to everything he asked of her.

She was very experienced at the art of loving and finally, when she realised that he was beginning to draw away, she became frantic.

She realised then that she loved the Earl as she had never loved anyone else in the whole of her life.

Her marriage had been arranged for her by her parents and, as she had been extremely gratified and delighted to be the Marchioness of Claydon, she had never found any pleasure in the more intimate moments of marriage.

It was only when, after giving her husband two sons and a daughter, she had taken her first lover that she discovered passion.

After that she had realised what she had been missing.

Even then she had never really been in love until she met the Earl.

Then, having fallen so deeply in love that she had the greatest difficulty in not begging him on her knees to run away with her, she had realised that she was just living in a 'Fool's Paradise'.

That Lady Esme should have supplanted her made it, she thought, even more bitter than if it had been some unknown beauty who did not belong to the same circle they inevitably saw each other almost every day and every evening.

The Prince of Wales had begun to enjoy a new freedom in the last few years.

He had gathered round him the younger and more amusing members of London Society and certainly the richest and the most raffish.

He had been married to the exquisitely beautiful Alexandra of Denmark in 1863, but by the summer of 1868, when their third child, Princess Victoria, was born, his love affairs had grown too numerous to be hushed up or ignored.

Two years earlier, when he was visiting St. Petersburg to attend the Wedding of Princess Alexandra's sister, Dagmar, to the Czarevitch

Alexander, there already were whispers that he was doing more than just flirting with the alluring beauties of the Russian Capital.

More tales trickled back from Paris, which he visited, again by himself, the following year.

And from then on, his conquests, or what was described as his 'troupe of fine ladies', followed one another in quick succession.

The first of many actresses in his life was the alluring Hortense Schneider. And after her there were beautiful women ranging from *debutantes* whom he saw at Presentation Balls to mature married beauties in the *Beau Monde*.

When the Prince of Wales then set the pace, a very different one from what his father and mother had considered conformable, who was not ready to follow him?

What was more, as one cynic remarked,

"Having invented infidelity, the Prince of Wales is now overwhelmed by it."

If the primrose path was made very easy for the Heir to the Throne, it likewise became increasingly easier for other gentlemen who up to now had led outwardly most circumspect lives.

Indeed, until the Prince Consort died, at even a breath of scandal they had always been liable to be scolded and more or less ostracised from Court.

Now the barriers were truly well down and so the Prince of Wales's love affairs were openly accepted, except by some of the more strait-laced families like that of the Marquis of Salisbury.

So everything became far easier and considerably more pleasant for the aristocrats of the Prince's age and those who were a little older.

But this did not make it any easier for the Marchioness of Claydon to accept that, to put it bluntly, the Earl of Sherburn was bored with her.

She had tried to delude herself into believing that it was just a transitory mood and he would return to her.

But the intervals between his visits became longer and longer and his explanations that he had other pressing business to attend to were not convincing.

When it became clear that 'business' was Lady Esme Meldrum, the Marchioness's anger and jealousy were almost uncontainable.

Never in her whole life had she hated anybody as much as she hated Lady Esme.

She would stare in the mirror for hours, wondering why her beauty had failed to hold the Earl when, in the opinion of most people, with her dark hair, flashing eyes and distinguished features, she was far more attractive than her rival.

But at last she had to accept that the Earl had gone and for the last month she had not seen him until they had met today with all the other guests at Alchester Castle.

It had given her a terrible shock when he had come into the salon before dinner and to the Marchioness's considerable annoyance her heart had turned a somersault and she had found it hard to breathe.

She had been very severe with herself during the last few weeks. .

Her pride had told her not to whine as so many other women had done when they lost the Earl and she had determined to pretend, even if nobody believed her, that she had been the first to bring their affair to an end because he no longer amused her.

The Marchioness might have had many faults, but she was not the type of woman to be crushed by adversity or to weep and wail even if she had lost what mattered most to her in life.

She told herself that she would fight and go on fighting and, even if in the end she did not get the Earl back, she would somehow make him sorry for the way he had treated her.

Sooner or later, she thought, she would take her revenge on Esme Meldrum as well and make her suffer as she was suffering.

Perhaps back in the Marchioness's antecedents there was an Italian or a Spanish ancestor who understood what was meant by a vendetta.

All of the Earl's other discarded women had wept helplessly, but had done nothing else.

The Marchioness was determined that she would be different.

'I will punish him,' she told her reflection in the mirror, 'if it is the last thing I ever do.'

She would lie awake at night thinking of the misfortunes and disasters she would inflict upon the Earl, until one day he would crawl back to her on his hands and knees and beg for mercy.

It was a fantasy that for a few moments at any rate assuaged the pain of her loss, which was like a physical wound in her heart.

Now, as she watched him walk into the salon and greet the Prince, she knew that no man had ever made her feel as he had when he kissed her.

She despised herself for knowing that if at this moment he held out his arms to her, she would run towards him like a homing pigeon.

Instead, holding herself tightly erect, she said as he approached her,

"Good evening, Osmond. It is delightful to see you again."

"There is no need for me to tell you that you are more beautiful than ever," the Earl replied lightly.

His voice sounded as if he was speaking sincerely, but the expression in his eyes told the Marchioness what she already knew, that he no longer had any interest in her and she hated him anew.

With an effort, because it was difficult to find her voice, she then replied,

"George is so looking forward to seeing you and let me introduce you to George's niece, poor Peter's daughter, who has just come to live with us."

As she spoke, she indicated a girl standing by her side, who was obviously very young and self-effacing.

"Forella," the Marchioness continued, "this is the Earl of Sherburn, who owns the finest racehorses in England and is also renowned as a great sportsman."

The Marchioness made the description sound almost an insult and the Earl, appreciating that she was being sarcastic, merely bowed to her niece and moved towards Lady Esme, who was standing at the other side of the room.

The way she held out her hand and the expression in her eyes as she looked at him told the Marchioness all too clearly what she already knew.

There was murder in her heart as she turned with an exaggerated effusiveness to greet another of her fellow guests.

*

Standing beside her aunt, Forella wondered why she was so angry.

In the strange life that she had lived with her father, Forella had learnt not only to judge people by what they said and how they looked but to feel the vibrations that came from them.

She was well aware as soon as she arrived a week ago at her uncle's house in Park Lane that her aunt was not at all pleased to see her.

She realised that the Marchioness was resenting with every nerve in her body that, since she had no other home, she was to live with them.

Although Forella had not been present at the arguments over what should be done about her, she was perceptively aware.

From the moment she had arrived from Italy, where her father had died in Naples during an epidemic of typhoid, she knew that, as far as her aunt was concerned, she was unwelcome.

"So are you telling me, George," the Marchioness had asked incredulously, "that your brother's child, whom I have never even seen, is to live with us? And I must present her at Court and bring her out as a *debutante*?"

"There is nothing else we can do, Kathie," the Marquis had replied sharply. "Now that Peter is dead, I am the girl's Guardian and, as she is nearly nineteen, she should have made her debut a year ago."

"That was always unlikely to happen whilst she was rampaging around the world with her eccentric father," the Marchioness replied harshly.

"I am aware of that," the Marquis said, "but, if Peter liked to lead his life his way, it was no business of ours. But now that he is dead, we have to do what is right and proper for his daughter."

"She must have other relations who would be only too glad to take care of her if you paid them enough money to do so."

"They are not in the same position as we are," the Marquis answered, "and I consider her my responsibility until she marries."

There was a poinant silence.

Then the Marchioness exclaimed,

"What you are really saying is that I have to find her a husband!"

"Why not?" the Marquis asked. "You have plenty of eligible nincompoops hanging about the place, drinking my wine and availing themselves of my hospitality. Surely one of them would be suitable to marry my niece?"

"With no dowry?" the Marchioness asked scathingly. "And I imagine, after the life she led with your brother, with very few social graces."

"She is an exceedingly pretty girl," the Marquis replied, "and I suppose you can smarten her up and teach her what she needs to know."

His wife did not reply and after a moment he said in a more conciliatory tone,

"Come on, Kathie, you were young yourself not so long ago and we can hardly leave the girl sitting in some slum in Naples with nobody to look after her except Peter's servant, who has travelled with him all through the years."

"You are not expecting to bring him here as well?" the Marchioness enquired.

"No, I intend to pension him off," the Marquis replied. "He is a good man and the least I can do is to give him a cottage in the country."

There was another silence for a moment.

Then the Marchioness queried,

"And the girl?"

"She will be arriving in three weeks' time. I have arranged for a Nun and a Courier to bring her over France. I thought it only right that she should have time to get over her father's death."

The word 'death' seemed to offer a speck of light to the Marchioness in the darkness of what her husband was asking her to do.

"If Forella is in mourning, she can hardly expect to attend balls and nobody wants a little black crow at any party."

"That is something that need not trouble you," the Marquis replied.

"Why not?" his wife enquired.

"Because Peter, who, as you know, was always unconventional, left a note in his Will to the effect that nobody was to mourn for him, nobody was to wear black and he wished to be buried quietly without any fuss."

The Marquis paused.

Then he added,

"My brother wrote to me,

"*I have had a damned good life and have enjoyed every moment of it. If anybody misses me, then I do hope that they will drink a glass of champagne to my memory and wish me luck wherever I may be in the future.*"

There was then a little break in the Marquis's voice as he repeated what his brother had written, but the Marchioness merely snorted.

"It sounds just the sort of nonsense your brother would write," she said, "but I suppose it makes it easier for me to do what you wish about his child. At the same time, George, do not think it will be easy for me, because it will not be!"

"What you are saying," the Marquis replied, "is that you very much dislike the idea of having to chaperone a *debutante*. Because I am not a fool, I appreciate that, Kathie. So the best thing you can do is to get her married off quickly. Then she will be off your hands and mine."

He paused before he added,

"I will give her three hundred pounds a year, which should make it easier, and you can spend what you like in decking her out."

For the first time since he had started talking to her, the Marchioness's eyes were less stormy.

"That is unusually generous of you, George!"

"I was fond of Peter," the Marquis said reflectively, "and, although you may not believe it, I often envied him."

He did not say anything more, but left the room while the Marchioness stared after him in astonishment.

How could George, who had everything, a famous title, great wealth and a position both at Court and in Society, envy his brother?

She had not seen Peter Claye very often, but when she had, she had found him totally incomprehensible and, if she was honest, because she did not understand him, she disliked him.

Peter had been only the third son of the previous Marquis and he therefore had not the slightest chance of succeeding to the title.

By the time George had married and had a son, Peter had begun to live a very different life from the rest of his family.

It was, of course, traditional that the younger sons should have very little, while all the money and possessions were entailed onto the heir.

Therefore, knowing he could not live the social life that entertained and amused his two brothers, he had set off on his own to explore the world.

He had soon spent his small amount of capital and then had to rely on the allowance he received every six months from the family Solicitors.

It was enough to allow him to travel as he had wished and to marry and be exceedingly happy with a wife who enjoyed the same strange roving life that intrigued him.

Their only child, Forella, before she could walk had travelled over deserts on the back of a camel.

She was dragged up the sides of mountains and sailed in creaking ships across strange seas to places where an Englishman and woman were a rarity and where the natives either stared at them or threatened them.

Occasionally, when his wife compelled him, Peter Claye would sit down and write for the Royal Geographical Society of his journeys and the unusual things he had seen.

But, while he talked about writing a book, usually he was too busy living his life to the full to have the time to set it down on paper.

"I will do that when I am too old to put one foot in front of the other," he would say, laughing.

Then they would go off again to some other place which Peter thought would be exciting and which he then wished to visit.

To Forella it was all a vast kaleidoscope of colour, new people, strange customs and she found them as absorbing as her father did.

Only when her mother had died did she realise that he was now her responsibility and that she must look after him as he was obviously quite incapable of looking after her.

Never in his life had Peter Claye been able to worry about tomorrow.

His whole philosophy had been,

'Enjoy today for tomorrow may never come'.

It came to him when, desperately short of money, they had lodged in what was really the slums of Naples while he decided where they would go next.

They had been warned that there were a number of cases of typhoid in the City, but he had laughed.

"It may be dangerous, Papa," Forella had insisted.

"I am indestructible," he had boasted and a week later he had died.

It was Jackson, Peter's servant, who had had the sense to write to the Marquis.

When he told Forella what he had done, she was angry with him.

"Why did you do that?" she asked. "Uncle George has paid no attention to us for years. Why should he worry about me now?"

"He has to worry about you, Miss Forella," Jackson answered.

"Why?"

"Because now that your father's dead, God rest his soul, his Lordship's your Guardian and he's got to do somethin' about you."

Forella looked with troubled eyes at the wiry little man.

"What do you mean by that? I don't want anybody to look after me."

"Now look 'ere, Miss Forella," Jackson said. "Now that the Master's no longer with us, we've got to do what's right and proper and what your mother, lovely lady she were, would have wanted if she was alive."

"I don't know what you are saying," Forella replied.

But indeed she had known and it terrified her.

Two weeks later the Marquis arrived in Naples in answer to Jackson's letter.

Because he resembled her father in good looks and was extremely kind and unexpectedly understanding, Forella cried for the first time since her father had died.

"I miss him, Uncle George," she said. "He was such fun to be with and nothing will ever be the same again."

"I know, my dear," the Marquis replied, "but now you have to live a new sort of life and that means coming to England with me."

"Oh, no!" Forella exclaimed involuntarily.

"You do not like the idea?"

"It – it frightens me," Forella explained. "Papa used to laugh and tell me how smart and important you and Aunt Kathie were."

She paused before she went on,

"Sometimes we would read about you in a newspaper that was usually weeks old, when we were in Singapore or Hong Kong or somewhere like that and Papa would say,

"There you are, Forella, my brother George is lording it above them all and I am proud of him, very proud. But thank God I do not have to live his life, even if he is 'Monarch of all he surveys'!"

The Marquis laughed.

"I can hear Peter saying that. He always thought Society a joke."

There was silence.

Then Forella said in a very small voice,

"Please, Uncle George – could I not – stay here with Jackson?"

The Marquis took her hand in his.

"Now listen to me, Forella," he said. "Jackson is a very nice little man, but he is getting on in years, while you are young, very young, and you have all your life in front of you."

His fingers tightened comfortingly as he went on,

"Now that you have to become a lady in the full sense of the word. That is what is best for you and what I believe in his heart your father would have wanted for you."

Because Forella had the uneasy feeling that this was true, she could not find words to go on arguing with.

Although she tried to forget it, she could remember her mother saying when they were in some obscure and rather uncomfortable part of the world,

"When Forella is eighteen, we shall have to go back to England, darling, and give her a chance to enjoy all the things that you have given up and that I never wanted."

Listening, Forella had been quite certain that her father would say it was an absurd idea, but in fact he had replied,

"Can you really see us all dolled up at Buckingham Palace with Forella wearing those ridiculous white feathers on her head and trying to curtsey to the Queen without tripping up over her train?"

"Yes, I can," his wife had insisted firmly.

There had been a little pause.

And then her father had said,

"Anyway, if I have to suffer that discomfort, which will be far worse than anything we have found here, I shall at least be escorting the two most beautiful women ever to enter the Throne Room!"

Forella had never thought about that conversation again.

But now since he had died everything her father had said to her seemed to come vividly to her mind and she had not argued any further with the Marquis.

He had therefore made arrangements for her and Jackson to be escorted to London, as soon as they were clear of the quarantine that had been imposed on Naples since the epidemic of typhoid began.

Three weeks later she had arrived at Park Lane and had known the moment she saw her aunt that she was unwanted and unwelcome.

Nevertheless the Marchioness had done what was expected of her and, although Forella was not aware of it, she had taken to heart her husband's idea that the girl should be married as quickly as possible.

She had taken Forella to the best shops and provided her with gowns that she had never thought it possible she would own.

Her hair had been cut and shaped by the most skilful and expensive coiffeur in London and everything she had brought with her from Italy had been either thrown away or burnt.

'I am no longer myself,' Forella thought a dozen times, 'but a puppet with Aunt Kathie pulling the strings and making certain that I don't think for myself, let alone say anything that has not been approved by her first.'

Because her education had been most cosmopolitan, she had learnt a dozen languages in different parts of the world, could calculate in the same number of currencies and cook better than most chefs.

Now her aunt concentrated on having Forella taught to dance gracefully and a teacher of deportment had come every day to teach her how to walk into a room, to use a fan, to bow, to curtsey and to shake hands.

She learnt to sit so that she showed nothing of her ankles and as little as possible of the toes of her shoes.

Actually she had learnt many of the dances of the East in order to amuse her father. She had watched the Dance of the Seven Veils and, without understanding exactly what they were portraying, the exotic dance of the Ouled Nails.

Her teacher had therefore found her a very quick pupil, with a grace and suppleness that was different from the rather stiff, often gauche *debutantes* he had taught before.

Deportment had been just as easy.

"Shall I show you how the Japanese greet their visitors?" Forella had asked. "And this is how the South Sea Islanders do it."

When this made him recoil in horror, she had laughed at the expression on his face, until he laughed too and the Marchioness had then come into the room to demand why they were making so much noise.

By the time she was ready to attend her first ball of the Season, Forella felt that she had been transformed from a rough uncut stone into a finished and well-polished gem,

'And just as hard and uninteresting', she said to herself.

When she was allowed to meet some of her aunt's friends, she found that the best thing she could do was to keep silent.

She soon realised that they were not in the least interested in her, and in fact, girls in her position were expected to be seen and not heard.

Her aunt's feelings had not changed in the slightest since she had come to live with them in Park Lane, so Forella kept out of her way as much as she could.

Her uncle was always unfailingly kind and often, when he returned home from the House of Lords, she would slip into his study, where he relaxed and read the newspapers, to talk to him.

To her surprise he really was interested in her father's travels.

He would ask her to tell him the whole story of her father's attempt to find the source of the Nile and to explain to him how they had got on with the various tribes in the Sudan who were supposed to be hostile.

"Once or twice," Forella said with a smile, "Mama thought our last hour had come. But Papa was so clever with those people and, of course. he could speak their language, which made all the difference."

"I wonder where he acquired that gift," the Marquis said thoughtfully. "I was never very good myself, even at French. Those 'frogs' talk far too fast for me to understand a word they say!"

Forella laughed.

"Papa could make himself understood anywhere and Mama found every language easy after her own."

"Of course," the Marquis agreed, "but then she was a foreigner."

He did not mean to say it unkindly, but merely as if it was somewhat of a disadvantage.

Actually her aunt had made it clear that her mother's nationality should be forgotten if Forella was to be a success in the Social world.

"Foreigners, unless they are French or Royal, are really not very acceptable," she had said in a lofty tone. "Of course, Kings and Princes are a different thing altogether. At the same time we have to find you an English husband and forget that most unfortunately you are not yourself wholly English."

There was obviously no point in arguing, so Forella had merely said meekly,

"Yes, Aunt Kathie."

"It will be no use being too particular," the Marchioness had carried on. "You have, as your uncle's niece, that one great asset, but then unfortunately you do have not much money. Anyway, we will make the very best of the fact that you are a Claye and no one can deny that they are one of the most aristocratic families in the country."

Forella tried to forget how her father had laughed at snobs and those who climbed the social tree and again, because an answer was expected of her, she said meekly,

"Yes, Aunt Kathie."

She said 'yes' and 'no' to her partners at dinner when they spoke to her, who obviously found it was a bore to have a young girl next to them.

Usually they were soon well engrossed in flirting with the very much more sophisticated women on their other side.

It was, although Forella did not realise it, a great surprise for most of the people to find such a young girl at any party given by Prince János.

He had made it a rule for a long time that his parties should consist of his very special friends who were more or less of the same age as he.

The women might be slightly younger, but invariably they were married and therefore, as everybody had the same interests, the same jokes and moved in the same circles, there was no one to bore them or to make it a duty to be polite.

Usually the only exception at the Prince's parties was an older woman who played the hostess and took the place of his wife.

The Prince's wife was a mystery and he never spoke of her.

However, it was generally assumed that she preferred to live in Hungary, although one or two people who had been to that country and had made enquiries had been unable to learn anything about her.

As usual, an older woman, on this occasion the scintillating and witty Lady Roehampton, played the part of hostess.

She was universally popular and understood all the intrigues and the likes and dislikes of a party, which was expected in a really successful hostess.

In fact Lady Roehampton had exclaimed in horror when the Prince had told her that the Marquis had asked if he and his wife could bring his niece for the weekend.

"A young girl? My dear János, you must be crazy! She will be like a fish out of water."

"I realise that," the Prince replied, "but I found it impossible to refuse Claydon. After all, if you remember, it was George who proposed me for White's Club when I first came to England and also sponsored me when I wished to join the Jockey Club."

He smiled at his success since then and finished,

"I have always felt that I owe him a debt of gratitude and this is one way that I can repay it."

"I understand all that," Lady Roehampton replied. "At the same time a young girl! Oh, dear. What shall I do with her?"

"As I gather from George that she has just arrived from abroad and knows nothing of England, I should just forget her."

The Prince laughed before he added,

"If you ask me, she will just watch everything wide-eyed and then find the whole thing entirely incomprehensible as I am sure you would have done at that age."

"It is too long ago for me to remember," Lady Roehampton replied.

She put her hand on his arm.

"You are quite right, János, you could not have refused George. But I am prepared to wager that Kathie is furious at having to take a young girl everywhere with her."

"In which case I am sorry for the child," the Prince remarked.

"I suppose you realise," Lady Roehampton went on, "that Kathie has lost Osmond?"

The Prince started.

"Are you telling me their affair is over?"

"Of course it is, it ended about three weeks ago after you went to Paris. And I hear too, although I may be wrong, that Osmond is now *epris* with Esme Meldrum."

"Good Heavens!" the Prince exclaimed. "And they are coming here this weekend. You should have told me before."

Lady Roehampton spread out her hands in an expressive gesture.

"Why worry? They all have to meet sooner or later and besides it will give everybody else a great deal to talk about."

The Prince sighed.

"I hope you are right, but I have a good mind to ask Esme Meldrum and Richard to come another time."

"I think they would consider that an extremely rude thing to do," Lady Roehampton said. "Besides I am not sure I am right in thinking there is something between Esme and Richard."

She wrinkled her brow and continued,

"It is just a whisper at the moment, yet I suppose that it was inevitable that Esme would attract Osmond's roving eye and he would find that pink-and-white Dresden china look of hers irresistible."

"Of course – irresistible!" the Prince agreed.

Lady Roehampton looked at him sharply.

"Do you mean – are you telling me, János – ?"

"No, no!" the Prince replied. "That would complicate things even more than they are already."

There was a smile on his face as he then walked away and, looking after him, Lady Roehampton wondered if any woman would ever capture the heart of János Kovác.

Knowing him as well as she did, she still found him an enigma, still unpredictable, still the man who she thought in her old age was far more attractive and intriguing than any other man she had ever met in her long life.

However, she did not pretend to understand him and, as she thought about him, she had the strange feeling that he did not understand himself.

CHAPTER TWO

As soon as the gentlemen joined the ladies after dinner, the Earl, without making much effort to be discreet, gravitated towards Esme Meldrum.

He thought her beautiful as she stood against a background of exotic flowers, apparently looking out at the last rays of the setting sun.

The Prince, unlike most hosts, would never have the curtains drawn until night had actually fallen.

The candles were lit in the chandeliers in the salon and their reflections glittered on the diamonds round Esme's neck. But they were not as brilliant, the Earl thought, as the light in her eyes.

He was aware, being very experienced with women, that it was because she was looking at him that she appeared to be so very radiant and there was also an undeniable invitation in the soft smile on her lips.

For a short moment he stood looking at her without speaking. Then, when she appeared to question his silence, he said,

"I think we both know that, while you are watching the sunset, for us it is the prelude to dawn."

"Are you sure that is what you want it to be?" she enquired.

"As that is an unnecessary question, I shall answer it later," he said.

There was a little pause before he asked,

"Which room are you sleeping in?"

She gave him a glance which told him that just as he desired her she felt the same and he thought it a gift from the Gods that Sir Richard Meldrum was not arriving until tomorrow.

Quickly, before she could reply, he said,

"I think, as this place is large enough to house a whole Regiment, we had better follow the example set by the Prince of Wales."

Esme laughed and he laughed too.

They were both aware that, when the Prince made advances to a pretty girl in a house he was not very familiar with, he always suggested that she should identify her bedroom for him by placing a rose outside the door.

"Perhaps that would be wise," Esme agreed. "After all, although I think I am on the same floor as you, there are a great number of bedrooms and I would not like you to get lost."

The way she spoke told the Earl all he wished to know and he thought it would be wise now to move away from her.

He could join several other men who were discussing where they should play cards or he could gratify a dozen of the other ladies by his attention.

But, spoilt because he always had his own way, he decided there was only one person he wanted to talk to at this moment and so he stayed where he was.

Prince János, having indicated to his other guests that card tables were waiting for them in an adjoining room, looked round to see if he had left anyone out and saw the Marchioness of Claydon, shimmering in green sequins as she stood by the fireplace.

As he started to walk towards her, he realised that she was not watching his approach but was looking at two people talking together by the window.

The expression on her face and the anger in her eyes were so vivid that the Prince did not have to guess who was upsetting her.

Instead, with the tact he was famous for and his charm that was irresistible, he went up to her and, taking her hand in his, said,

"I do not have to tell you, Kathie, that you are the most beautiful woman here tonight and every time I see you I am convinced you grow lovelier."

For a moment the Marchioness's eyes widened with surprise.

The Prince had always been very courteous and delightful to her and she was extremely gratified that she and George were so often included in his parties.

However, he had never singled her out and, because he was so unpredictable, she had never considered even for a moment that he might become her lover.

She would, of course, have been thrilled if there was the slightest chance of it, for to capture the heart of Prince János Kovác would have been a feather in any woman's cap. But she had never given even a fleeting thought to anything so wildly improbable.

Now for the first time it flashed through her mind that, if he really found her attractive, he would certainly be a very adequate replacement for the Earl.

Half-closing her eyes and looking at him in the enigmatic manner that she had found in the past intrigued any man, she replied,

"Dear János, you are always so kind and I do wish I could believe that you are speaking truthfully."

"How can you doubt it?" the Prince asked. "And, Kathie, I have just bought a painting I should like your opinion on. I think it will amuse you because there is a certain resemblance in it to yourself."

Without waiting for the Marchioness to reply, he drew her from the salon and took her across the hall to an attractive sitting room where the painting he was referring to had been hung over the mantelpiece.

It was a portrait of an unknown Venetian woman painted in the early eighteenth Century.

She was not only very beautiful, but the Marchioness could see there was undoubtedly a faint resemblance to herself in the dark hair and the dark eyes of the sitter.

She was aware as she looked up, arching her neck to show what had often been called 'the exquisite outline' of it, that the Prince was watching her.

Then she said very softly,

"Thank you, János. At the same time you flatter me."

"How can I do that?" the Prince asked, "when you are well aware you are the belle of every ball you attend? I noticed that there was no one to touch you at Marlborough House the other night and I heard Prince Albert say the same thing,"

"Shall I pretend that you are making me feel shy?" the Marchioness enquired. "Or shall I ask you to tell me more?"

"It is something I am only too willing to do," the Prince replied, "but, as you well know, I must first look after my guests. All the same, Kathie, we have the whole weekend in front of us."

As he spoke, he took her hand in his and turned it over and kissed the palm.

It was a very graceful gesture and one that the Prince was extremely proficient at.

It made the Marchioness draw in her breath and, as they then walked hand-in-hand to the door, she was smiling and looking very different from the way she had in the salon.

The Prince escorted her to the card room and, sitting down at the Baccarat table where a number of the other guests were waiting for him to take the Bank, he put the Marchioness on his right, saying as he did so,

"I feel you will bring me luck, so tonight we will play together."

The Marchioness was delighted for she knew this meant that he would cover her losses, while any winnings that ensued would be hers.

However rich anybody was in the Social world, they were never too rich to refuse more.

The Marchioness was already thinking as they started to play that she might after all be able to buy the sable stole she wanted, which George had refused to give her on the grounds that it was too expensive.

Because the Prince was so rich and the majority of his guests were also very wealthy, the stakes at the Baccarat table were very high.

As a perfect host, Prince János usually contrived that those who could not afford to lose found themselves, without realising what was happening, seated at a Bridge table.

It was two hours later when the Marchioness's thoughts returned to the Earl and Esme Meldrum.

By that time the pile of gold coins in front of her at the Baccarat table had multiplied pleasingly.

Only as she lost at the last turn of the cards did she think that her luck had changed and she would be wise to move away while she was still a large winner.

As if the Prince realised what she was thinking, he suggested,

"I am sure you would like a glass of champagne. Shall we go and find one before I start a new shoe?"

"That would be delightful," the Marchioness replied.

They rose from the table and one of the guests asked quickly,

"You are not leaving, Kovác?"

"No, of course not," he replied. "Just stretching our legs and looking for something to quench our thirst."

"You might be allowed to drink a toast to yourself," came the reply, "but hurry back, I am determined to have my revenge."

"You shall have it," the Prince nodded good-humouredly.

He walked with the Marchioness into the salon next door and as he did so he was aware that seated on a sofa at the end of it were the Earl and Esme Meldrum, talking to each other intimately.

There were two other people in the room and the Marchioness saw with surprise that it was her husband with Forella beside him.

They too were talking animatedly and, as she and the Prince walked to them, Forella's laughter rang out spontaneously.

Because she looked so lovely and because at the same time the Marchioness was actually aware of how interested the Earl was in her rival, she had to find fault with somebody.

She therefore stopped beside her husband and said to Forella,

"I hoped by this time you would have had the sense to go to bed and not bother your poor uncle, who I am sure is longing to be at the card table where he usually is."

"That is just where you are mistaken," the Marquis replied before his niece could speak. "Forella and I have been having an extremely interesting talk and I am enjoying myself."

"I am glad to hear it," the Marchioness said obviously not really attending to what he was saying but looking out of the corner of her eye at the Earl on the other side of the room.

The Prince came from the side table where he had poured out two glasses of champagne. As he handed one to her, he asked,

"What about you, George? Shall I find you a drink?"

"Don't worry," the Marquis replied. "I will get one for myself. As a matter of fact your wines at dinner were so excellent that I am not thirsty."

"I hoped you would enjoy them."

It was then that the Marchioness realised that Forella, standing at her uncle's side, was waiting to say 'goodnight', but she deliberately turned her back to talk to the Prince.

Even so she could hear Forella say,

"Thank you, Uncle George, you have been so kind and I have enjoyed this evening more than I can tell you."

She kissed his cheek and then, obviously wishing to escape as soon as she could from her aunt's condemnation, moved quickly across the room towards the door.

As she did so, the Marchioness thought that the sooner she could get the girl married the better.

It was then, almost as if it was out of the blue, an idea came to her.

*

Once in the hall, Forella did not hurry, but then walked slowly up the magnificent carved staircase, thinking that The Castle was the finest building that she had ever seen and certainly the grandest she had ever stayed at.

She told herself that whatever anybody else did tomorrow, she would find someone to show her round and especially the paintings.

It was her mother who had been interested in art and had made her visit the Museums whenever they were in a City that had one.

She had also taught her to appreciate the beauties of the strange lands they visited.

"There is beauty everywhere, darling," she had said once, "and you do not have to own beauty to capture it for you can hold it in your mind so that whether you are rich or poor it is yours forever afterwards."

It was something that Forella had always remembered.

Now, walking along the corridor with its magnificent pieces of furniture, huge carved mirrors and paintings by old Masters, she told herself that it was all hers.

'The next time I am sleeping in a tent in the desert,' she thought, 'or in a confined cabin of some small smelly Steamship, I will conjure up what I am seeing now.'

Then she remembered with a pang in her heart that there would be no more voyages into the unknown, no more hardships and adventures, which were always so exciting in retrospect.

Instead there would be just the social life she was experiencing with her aunt and uncle and which she found at times dull and at others incomprehensible.

'They eat and talk, talk and eat, and that goes on day after day,' she thought. 'No wonder the men grow fat and the women catty.'

As she was extremely intelligent, although she was ignorant of the Social world, she had not missed the spiteful things her aunt often said about other women to her friends, to her husband and, when there was no one else around, to Forella as well.

She did not understand their jokes and all their innuendoes went over her head.

At the same time she knew that it was all very paltry and unimportant and she longed to be talking to her father about the customs of the Berbers or the significance of Mecca to a Moslem or planning with him an expedition that would take them into territory where very few other Europeans had ever ventured.

'Oh, Papa,' she cried out in her heart, 'why did you have to leave me?'

She realised as the question vibrated on the air that she had reached her bedroom and a maid was waiting to help her undress.

This was a luxury that she was not accorded to in her uncle's house in Park Lane and she said quickly,

"I am sorry. I should have told you not to wait up for me."

"It's my duty, miss," the maid replied rather primly.

"Do you not get very tired?" Forella asked her curiously.

"I sometimes get the chance, miss, of a little lie-down in the afternoon and it's only at weekends when the house is full that we have to keep goin' for so long."

She did not wait for Forella to answer but went on,

"You're early, miss. I don't suppose the rest of the party'll come up until nearly dawn."

Forella thought it was rather cruel especially for her aunt's maid, who she realised now would be waiting next door and was getting on in years.

Then she told herself that it was not for her to criticise.

As her maid then hung up her gown in the wardrobe, she walked across the room to the communicating door to be quite certain that it was tightly shut.

As she did so, she thought with a little smile that, if there was the slightest excuse for Aunt Kathie to complain, she would.

The room that Forella was sleeping in was very large and the huge bed draped with silk curtains was very impressive.

"I see you are next to your uncle and me," the Marchioness had said when they arrived "and I think it is very considerate of Lady Roehampton. Young girls are usually in single rooms in another part of The Castle."

The way she spoke made Forella feel that it was not so much a matter of congratulation as a reproof.

The Marchioness had made it very clear that it was very unusual for a young girl to be staying in any house party that consisted of older people like herself.

"Where Prince János is concerned," she had added, "it is unheard of for anybody he entertains to be so young."

Forella could not think of a reply so she remained silent.

"I hope you realise how fortunate you are," her aunt had finished in the hard voice in which she habitually addressed her.

"I am very grateful, Aunt Kathie."

"And so you should be. At least you will be able to hold your own, as far as concerns your clothes. Heaven knows what your uncle will say when he sees the bills!"

Forella had heard this remark so often before that it had ceased to impress her as it had done at first.

She had actually said to the Marquis when they were alone,

"Thank you, Uncle George, for being so very kind and generous in giving me so many beautiful gowns, but I am sure that I could do with fewer."

Her uncle had smiled and patted her shoulder.

"You are very pretty, my dear, and clothes are important to a woman."

"I know they are, but they are also very expensive."

"You will not bankrupt me," he had said with a smile.

"And when, as I most undoubtedly will, take you up the aisle to be married to somebody of high standing, it will give me great pleasure."

Forella knew that by 'high standing' he meant somebody in the same Society in which they themselves moved.

She longed to reply to her that she would much rather marry an explorer or a foreigner and knew how horrified her aunt would be at such an admission.

Ever since she had reached London she had had it drummed into her day after day by her aunt that her father's way of life had been eccentric to the point of being outrageous and that she was extremely fortunate to have been saved from it.

It was impossible to protest in reply that she lay awake at night hating the softness of her bed, disliking the feeling of being confined between four walls and longing instead for the wide open spaces under a star-studded sky.

She yearned too for the turbulent waves of a strange sea moving beneath her.

'Aunt Kathie would never understand,' she thought despairingly and knew that there was no point in trying to tell anybody what she felt.

Now she drew back the heavy brocade curtains, pulled up the dark blinds and, opening all the windows, let in the night air.

It felt cool and refreshing after the heat of the rooms downstairs and Forella leant out.

There were stars overhead, but they were not as brilliant or as numerous as those that had shone over her in the East.

But there was enough light from the moon coming up the sky to see its reflection on the lake which lay in front of the house, and to be able to discern the ancient oak trees in the Park on the far side of it.

'If only Papa was here,' she told herself, 'he would help me to study the history of The Castle and to appreciate its treasures. At the same time he would laugh at the people who are staying in it and refuse to take them in any way seriously.'

She told herself that she must do the same and that she had been feeling so depressed as she was taking her new life with her uncle and aunt more seriously than was necessary.

'It is just an uncomfortable phase in my life,' she told herself, 'like climbing a .mountain with a blistered foot or sleeping in some of those little dak bungalows in India that had snakes in the rafters."

She could remember a time in Turkey when she and her father and mother had been caught in a terrible storm and had to shelter in a cave which smelt strongly of wild animals.

After they had been there for a short time they had begun to itch from the bites of insects that the animals had left behind them.

She remembered that her father had sworn vigorously as he scratched himself and, when her mother had rebuked him laughingly, he had said,

"A few good British swear words never hurt anyone. I can only hope the damned fleas understand English!"

They all had laughed and after that it had seemed a tremendous joke.

'I have to laugh at everything that is happening to me,' Forella told herself.

She climbed into bed to lie gazing at the stars until she finally fell asleep.

*

Forella was dreaming that she was with her father when she was awakened by the sound of the door opening.

Because she had so often slept in very odd places, she was a very light sleeper and had learnt to wake to the rustle of a cobra slithering over the floor or the snorting of a wild animal outside.

Then she was aware to her surprise that there was somebody just inside the door.

She could not see who it was because the light that came through her windows from the moon and stars did not penetrate that far.

Although she was aware that there was somebody there, being still half-asleep she was not for the moment afraid.

Then, as the tall figure of a man began to cross the room to the bed, she gave a little gasp and tried to ask,

"Who are – you? What do you – want?"

He said distinctly in a low voice,

"Esme?"

It was then as she opened her mouth to scream that the door of the communicating room opened and her aunt came into the room, carrying a silver candelabrum with lit candles.

She was wearing an elaborate *negligée* of satin and lace and looked, Forella thought, most imposing and undeniably beautiful.

However she was looking not at her but at the man standing beside the bed with his back to the window.

Now Forella saw that it was the Earl of Sherburn who had frightened her.

As she looked at him, she was aware that he was staring at her in utter astonishment and at the same time he seemed to be turned to stone.

The Marchioness's eyes met his across the room.

Then she said in a clear tone which seemed to ring out in the silence,

"Really, Osmond, how can you do anything quite so outrageous as to attempt to seduce someone as young as Forella?"

For a moment it seemed as if the Earl found it impossible to speak.

Then at last he said,

"I am, of course, in the wrong room."

"You can hardly expect me to believe that!" the Marchioness replied.

She spoke mockingly and Forella thought that there was an unpleasant smile, as it were of triumph, on her lips.

She turned her head to call out,

"George, will you come here immediately? I told you there was somebody in Forella's bedroom."

As if her words galvanised the Earl into action, he walked away from the side of the bed to the centre of the room to confront the Marchioness.

Although he spoke in a lowered voice, it was possible for Forella to hear what he said.

"You are well aware, Kathie, of the truth of the matter and it would be a great mistake for you to make a scene!"

"I am aware of nothing of the sort," the Marchioness replied.

She had answered him in the same lowered voice that he had used.

Then, as if without turning round she was aware that her husband had come into the room and was standing just behind her, she said,

"I can imagine nothing more disgraceful than that I should find you here!"

"What is all this about? What is going on?" the Marquis demanded.

"You may well ask, George," his wife replied. "I heard a sound, as I told you. So I came to investigate and found Osmond at Forella s bedside!"

The Marquis for the moment seemed stunned.

"What is this all about, Sherburn?" he asserted. "You have never met the girl until this evening!"

The Marchioness gave a very unpleasant laugh.

"For all we know, George, they may have been meeting each other in London or else Osmond suddenly has developed a penchant for cradle-snatching. Anyway the point is what are you going to do about it?"

"What do you mean?" the Marquis asked.

Then, as if he was suddenly aware that something more was expected of him, he said,

"I suppose, Sherburn, you should apologise."

"I have already explained," the Earl replied, "that I made a mistake in coming into the wrong room. I expect you to believe me, George, even if your wife does not."

" "Well, of course, if – " the Marquis began, but the Marchioness interrupted him.

"My dear George, you must be aware that in the circumstances the only thing our good friend the Earl of Sherburn can do is to behave honourably. You cannot allow your niece's reputation to be dragged in the mud without his making the obvious reparation."

"Good God, you cannot mean – ?" the Marquis asked.

"I mean," the Marchioness said decisively, "that the very least Osmond can do in all the circumstances is to offer Forella marriage!"

There was a silence after she had spoken and the Earl held his breath.

Then Forella, who had sat up in bed without being aware of it, cried,

"No, *no*! Of course – not! It was a – mistake, Aunt Kathie. Of course it was a – mistake."

As she spoke, she remembered that, while she was chatting to her uncle, she had seen the Earl talking to the beautiful Lady Meldrum on the sofa and had thought rather vaguely how attractive they looked together.

It was almost, she told herself, as if they were the hero and heroine in a play.

Although she could not hear what they said, she was aware that the Earl was flirting with Lady Esme and she was flirting with him with her eyes, her lips and the little gestures that she made with her hands.

It was so fascinating that Forella had wanted to watch them, but she knew it would be embarrassing if they realised that she was staring at them.

She had therefore forced herself not to look more than she could help in their direction, but to keep her eyes on her uncle.

Now, of course, she understood that the Earl had wanted to be alone with Lady Esme, which he could not be downstairs.

He had therefore intended to go to her bedroom and doubtless she had been expecting him, but by mistake he had come into Forella's.

As she spoke, the Marchioness turned to her with an unmistakable expression of anger in her eyes as she said,

"You be quiet! Doubtless you are as much to blame for this immoral behaviour as he is! Let me point out, Forella, that no man would have come to your bedroom unless you had encouraged him!"

Her aunt's attack was so astonishing that for a moment Forella could only stare at her open-mouthed.

Then, as she tried to find words to express her own innocence in, the Marquis said,

"I suppose, Sherburn, the only thing you can do in the circumstances is to make the best of it. After all I cannot have my niece's reputation soiled by scandal at her age."

Again there was silence and Forella, looking apprehensively at the Earl, thought that she had never seen a man look so grim and at the same time so contemptuous.

He was looking not at her uncle but at her aunt as he said,

"Very well, you win! I will marry your niece and I hope she enjoys being my wife!"

His words seemed to vibrate round the room.

Then, as he finished speaking, he walked to the door and pulled it open and, as he went out, he slammed it behind him.

Forella found her voice again.

"No – please – Uncle George. It is all a – terrible mistake – " she began.

"I daresay that is the truth," the Marquis interrupted, "but your aunt is right. You cannot afford to have your reputation smeared before you have even been presented."

As he finished speaking, he walked out through the communicating door into his own bedroom and Forella watched him go with a feeling of despair.

"Wait – please wait – Uncle George – !" she cried.

The Marchioness walked to the foot of the bed to say,

"Shut up and don't be such a little fool! I have found you a husband whom most girls would go on their knees to marry and, although he will doubtless lead you a hell of a life, you will be the Countess of Sherburn!"

She seemed almost to spit the words at Forella.

Then, as if she could not bear the sight of her, she turned away abruptly and followed her husband, taking the candelabrum with her.

Forella gave a little cry of sheer horror.

She could hardly believe it had all happened and she felt that she must still be dreaming and this was a nightmare.

Then she knew that it was impossible, completely and absolutely impossible, for her to be married to a man she did not know and had met for only one brief second and who she was well aware was in love with somebody else.

'I cannot do it! Oh, Papa, *save me*!' she prayed.

Getting out of bed, she walked to the window to stand gazing at the stars.

*

Having reached his own bedroom, the Earl was feeling very much the same as Forella was, as if he had stepped into a nightmare that he could not extricate himself from.

He understood only too well what had actually happened and, after everyone had gone to bed, Kathie must have looked to see if there was a rose outside Esme's bedroom.

Looking back now into the past, he remembered how on one occasion they had laughed together about the Prince's arrangement with a woman who had taken his fancy.

Therefore it was obvious that Kathie had guessed that tonight he would use that means of identifying Esmie's bedroom.

'It was revenge,' he told himself, 'that was too severe for the crime.'

After all no *affaire de coeur* he was involved in lasted for very long and it was unusual for the women he left, generally in tears, to become his enemies.

He always tried to make them friends in the same way as the Prince of Wales managed to do.

It was well known that, when one of his love affairs ended, he was invariably loyal to the lady in question as she had been loyal to him.

But where the Earl was concerned there had been unfortunate moments in the past when the lady in whom he was no longer interested had made a scene and had threatened him.

But never had any such threat, however dramatic, ever been put into operation.

Now he thought that the Marchioness had succeeded where the others had failed and for the moment he could not think how he could extricate himself from a situation that was not only intolerable but exceedingly humiliating.

He had no wish, at least not for many years, to marry anybody least of all, he thought savagely, a very young girl who might make him a submissive wife but with whom he would be bored stiff within a month of their marriage or even earlier.

What was more, every instinct in him resented being pressurised into marriage or, to put it bluntly, caught as he had just been.

'I will not do it! I am damned if I will!' he told himself.

But, as he flung himself down on his bed, he felt that it might as well be a bed of nails and he could not imagine what he could do to escape from this burden.

The Marchioness held every trump card and had certainly played them.

In the meantime he was aware that, if he was to take any action to free himself, he would have to act quickly.

He was certain that Kathie would tomorrow inform Lady Roehampton, if not the Prince, that he had proposed to Forella.

For the girl's sake, she would not specify in what circumstances. But, if he knew the way her brain worked, she would probably insinuate that they had been meeting in London ever since Forella had arrived from Naples.

She would then say that he had seized the opportunity last night when they were all at The Castle to inform her aunt and uncle of his intentions.

There would be doubts concerning the truth of this in the minds of a number of people who had observed his behaviour with Esme Meldrum.

However, they would be very delighted that having been elusive for so long he had been caught in the bonds of matrimony, 'bonds' being definitely the right word for it.

He could almost hear their gushing congratulations and their cynical good wishes for his future happiness.

'What the devil can I do?' he asked himself aloud in the darkness.

It flashed through his mind that he might go abroad, but that would solve nothing for he could not stay away indefinitely.

He knew without even thinking on it that to appeal to Forella was hopeless, as she would inevitably be overruled by her aunt and uncle.

He did not have even to consider how delighted Kathie would be not to have a young girl clinging onto her.

The Earl was extremely knowledgeable in the psychology of women and he had known immediately on hearing from some gossip-monger that George Claydon had a niece coming out this Season that Kathie would be furious.

"I hate young girls!" she had said to him once when they were together. "I just cannot imagine how they could ever turn into amusing and witty women!"

'You must have been very young yourself once,' he had said mockingly.

"Never!" Kathie had exclaimed. "I was born old and wise in everything that mattered and with a knowledge of witchcraft, which you yourself have complained about."

"Of course, " the Earl had agreed. "You bewitched me from the first moment I saw you."

It was the answer she wanted and, as her arms went round his neck and he felt her body moving against his, he had told himself that she held an enchantment he found irresistible.

But witches could be very dangerous and he realised that he should never have become involved with Kathie in the first place.

He had always preferred fair women with blue eyes who were usually rather stupid.

While the Marchioness was undoubtedly one of the most beautiful women he had ever seen, her black hair and eyes should have warned him that she could be deeply revengeful and implacably dangerous as he now knew to his cost.

But it was too late.

He had walked into the trap that she had set for him and no amount of struggling would get him out of it.

CHAPTER THREE

The Prince always woke up early in the morning and usually went out riding at about six o'clock.

This morning, however, when he opened his eyes and saw the sun streaming in through the open window, it was an hour earlier.

He had gone to bed with a certain worry on his mind that was still there for his instinct, which because of his Hungarian blood was unusually perceptive, had told him that something was wrong.

He was not certain what it was, except that he thought it concerned the Marchioness and Lady Esme.

But a red flag was being waved in front of him and nothing could stop him from feeling this weird and unaccountable apprehension.

Because, whenever he woke, he needed to become active, he got up and dressed himself without ringing for his valet and walked downstairs and out towards the stables.

By this time a few of the younger housemaids in mob caps and gingham dresses were beginning to pull back the curtains and clean out the grates.

There were also, the Prince was aware, footmen in their shirtsleeves clearing away the glasses from where they had been left in the salon and card room.

Later the older servants would be appearing to supervise them and give instructions to ensure that everything was in perfect order by the time he or his guests appeared.

The fact that he was unusually early caused the servants to give him quick questioning glances as if they felt too that something must be wrong.

But the Prince walked purposefully to the stables, feeling that what he wanted more than anything else was to ride one of his most spirited horses.

He would then enjoy a battle for supremacy in which he was invariably the victor, but he would have the satisfaction of knowing that he had been forced to fight for it.

He regularly brought over from Hungary horses that were only half-trained and he knew that his experience with horseflesh was admired not only by his friends but by everybody he employed.

He then reached the stables, which since he had bought The Castle, had been completely rebuilt.

He congratulated himself not only on the architect's skill in designing the new building to match the architecture of The Castle, especially the Georgian part of it, but also that his horses were housed in greater comfort than those of any other owner in the country.

Because he was so early, there was only a stable boy on duty, who gave him a startled glance and then hurried to alert the Head Groom.

The Prince moved down the long line of stalls, deciding which horse he would ride and seeing with pleasure that one that had arrived only the previous week from Hungary had now settled down.

At least he was no longer fighting for freedom or attempting to kick down his stall as he had done on arrival.

Because his own feelings were somewhat disturbed this morning, the Prince decided that he would ride Aspád as this fine horse had been named.

He was about to open the stable door of his stall when, breathing heavily from the speed he had hurried with, his Head Groom joined him.

"Good mornin', Your 'Ighness," he said respectfully. "I wasn't expectin' you so early."

"I know, Barton," he replied, "but it is a lovely morning and I do need some exercise."

He knew as he spoke that all his servants thought it extraordinary that, however late he went to bed, he was always up early and as active and energetic as if he had had eight hours' deep sleep.

The Prince had trained himself to keep his body as strictly under control as his emotions.

He found that when it suited him he could do quite well with three hours sleep when other men needed double that amount.

"I was thinking, Barton," he said, "that I might ride Aspád this morning. I can see he is far quieter than he was when he arrived."

"That he be, Your 'Ighness," his Head Groom replied, "and a finer 'orse I've never seen. Once Your 'Ighness has trained 'im, he'll be superb."

"That is what I thought myself," the Prince replied.

He stepped back for Barton to open the door of the stall, but to his surprise the groom paused.

The Prince saw that there was a frown between his eyes.

"What is it?" he asked.

"I've only just bin told, Your 'Ighness," Barton answered him, "that one of the guests was 'ere this mornin' and, as only Jeb was on duty and he's a rather stupid boy, she insisted on ridin' off on Gyõrgy."

The Prince stared at him in astonishment.

"Gyõrgy!" he exclaimed.

"Yes, Your 'Ighness. Of course, if I'd a-knowed, I wouldn't have allowed it. Gyõrgy is a good 'orse, as Your 'Ighness knows, but he ain't the right mount for a lady."

The Prince knew that this was true.

Gyõrgy was the last horse he had broken in himself, but was still very wild and at times almost uncontrollable and he knew that Barton was right when he said that he was certainly not a mount for any woman however experienced.

"I think there must be some mistake, Barton," he said. "Did Jeb say who it was who had asked for Gyõrgy?"

"He didn't know 'er name, Your Highness," Barton replied, "but he said she were very pretty and much younger than Your Highness's guests usually be."

"Saddle Jóska quickly while I find out from Jeb the direction the lady has gone."

The Prince strode off and Barton hurried to Jóska's stall, realising that the Prince knew that he had no time to struggle with Aspád.

Jóska, who was one of the fastest and largest horses in the whole stable, would carry him wherever he wanted to go quicker than any of the others.

The Prince found Jeb carrying in a pail of water from the yard.

Jeb looked at his Master apprehensively having guessed from what Barton had said to him that he had done something wrong.

"Have you any idea, Jeb, " the Prince asked calmly, "in which direction Miss Claye, who is riding Gyõrgy, has gone?"

"Aye, Your 'Ighness."

Jeb put down the pail and pointed towards the far end of the Park.

"I watched 'er go, Your 'Ighness," he explained, "and, as Gyõrgy were playin' up, I were afraid 'e might throw 'er, but 'er rode 'im as if she knew what she were a-doin'."

"I hope she does," the Prince muttered beneath his breath.

He turned to where Barton was bringing Jóska out from his stable and into the yard.

He mounted quickly and, as the huge black stallion started pulling at the reins, eager to be off, he rode him swiftly across the Park in the direction that Jeb had pointed to.

As he went, he thought it inconceivable that any young girl should have chosen Gyõrgy to ride and thinking herself capable of handling a horse that had given him so much trouble.

György was not only very hard to control but was also inclined to shy at anything that he considered unusual.

The Prince imagined that he would find Miss Claye, he could not recall her first name, lying unconscious somewhere on the ground and that when he had carried her home he would have to send the grooms in search of György.

He had never thought, never guessed, that anyone wanting to ride his horses would be up so early that Barton would not be there to advise them and prevent any horse that was unsafe from being taken from the stables.

He realised that it was because Jeb was so stupid that he had not awakened Barton to ask his advice and to tell him that the Claye girl, obviously pleased with the horse's looks, had asked to ride him.

When he thought about her, he tried to remember what she was like. At least he was sure that she did not in any way appear to be a 'horsy' type.

He could only hope that when György did throw her, which would undoubtedly happen as quickly as possible, she would fall on soft ground, preferably in the meadowland where it was unlikely that she would break any bones.

It would, however, cause a commotion and upset his house party. And he would have to apologise to the Marquis because, through no fault of his own, one of his horses had injured his niece.

The Prince reached the end of the Park then, giving Jóska his head, galloped across a flat piece of land, which the stallion took at a speed that would not have been rivalled on any Racecourse.

The Prince was making for the high ground at the far end from which he could look for several miles over a valley that a small stream ran through.

Reining in Jóska, he made him take the sharp incline more slowly and when they reached the top he came to a standstill.

He looked first near at hand, expecting to see a still body on the ground and doubtless Gyõrgy careening wildly some distance away.

But there was no sign of either of them and, when he looked further ahead through the trees towards the stream, then a good two miles away, he saw them.

To his surprise the girl was still in the saddle and was riding Gyõrgy along the side of the stream.

It looked as if she was trying to find a place to cross it, although why she should wish to do so he had no idea.

However, there had been a considerable amount of rain during the last month or so and the stream, usually quite shallow, was swollen to double its usual size.

Now that he had seen her, the Prince did not waste time speculating what she was about to do, but knew that the sooner he reached her the better.

He moved down the incline and, having once again given Jóska his head, he set off at a pace that brought him down into the valley and only a short distance from Forella in a little over fifteen minutes.

She was still moving along the bank of the stream, trying to find a suitable place to cross it. She had reasoned out that because London was North of them, it would be best for her to go South.

Although she was completely ignorant of the English countryside and of the extent of the Prince's estate, she thought that the land on the other side of the water looked wilder and less cultivated.

She was obsessed with only one idea, and that was to get away, and she knew she had been extremely lucky in being able to ride a horse that had, she was sure, both the strength and the endurance to carry her all day.

She had to draw György to a sharp standstill where for the first time she could see to the bottom of the stream and she knew that at this point it was not so very deep and a horse could wade across it easily.

She turned him towards the water and, as she did so, she looked back.

It was then that she saw, still some distance away, a man approaching her on horseback.

Instantly she was aware that she was in danger and, without riding any further on into the stream, she turned György back in the direction they had been riding before and spurred him.

Then György was only too willing to show off his paces.

But to demonstrate his independence, he at first reared up, hoping his rider would fall off his back and, when she did not, he bucked two or three times before, obedient to the spur in his side, he set off at a wild gallop.

Watching, the Prince held his breath as the horse bucked, expecting to see Forella crash to the ground.

He also knew how easy it was for an inexperienced rider to be unseated by a horse that was bucking.

When he saw Forella, still in the saddle, set off in what he knew was a deliberate effort to avoid him, he thought it a miracle.

This, however, was a challenge to Jóska that he could not ignore.

There was no need for the Prince even to touch him lightly with his whip or to use his spurs.

Instead the stallion leapt on forward and there was the thunder of his hoofs as he strained every nerve to show his supremacy by overtaking the horse in front of him.

As she heard the Prince approaching, Forella could hardly believe that any animal could outpace the one she was riding.

But however much she urged György on, she could still hear the man behind her coming nearer and nearer until at last she knew despairingly that she could not escape.

She went on trying, however, until at last the Prince on Jóska drew up alongside her and she realised who had been following her.

It was such a relief to see that it was only the Prince and not, as she had expected, the Marquis, who would have been sent by her aunt to bring her back.

Because there was no point in going on racing, she gradually and, as the Prince noticed without any difficulty, drew Gyõrgy to a trot, then to a walk and the Prince did the same with Jóska.

After the speed at which they had been riding, even he was a little breathless as he asked a very different question from the one he had intended.

"Where in God's name did you learn to ride like that?"

Because it was so unexpected, Forella gave a little laugh.

"Gyõrgy is magnificent! I saw his name over his stall, so I know he was from Hungary."

"Of course," the Prince replied. "But I would be interested to know, Miss Claye, where you are going with him."

Forella was about to say that she was going nowhere in particular, when she was aware that the Prince had seen the rolled-up bundle at the back of her saddle.

There was not much in it, but she had thought that she could not leave with absolutely nothing of her own.

Because Jeb had not understood what she wanted, she had herself, with some difficulty because Gyõrgy had been restless, attached it to the saddle.

It was something she was expert at doing, having so often had to pack almost everything she possessed onto a horse, a mule or a camel when she was travelling with her father.

There was a brush and a comb in one saddle-pocket and a toothbrush, a sponge and a piece of soap in the other.

Because she was used to travelling light, she knew that for a short while at any rate she would not have to buy such necessities out of the very small amount of money she had with her.

Then, as she was wondering desperately what she could reply to the Prince, he said and she thought it was extraordinarily perceptive of him,

"If you are running away, as I suspect you are, I think I am entitled to ask you, if nothing else, where you are taking my horse!"

He saw the colour flooding into her face before she replied in a low voice,

"I apologise for – stealing him, but I – swear to you I would have – returned him as soon as it was – possible for me to do so."

The Prince was silent for a moment.

Then he said,

"I wonder if we could talk about this. Although I cannot force you to confide in me, it is something I would ask you to do, if only for Gyõrgy's sake."

As the way he spoke was neither condemning nor disagreeable but seemed kind and, although she could not explain it, sympathetic, Forella said quickly,

"It would be much easier, Your Highness, if you would – pretend not to have seen me and let me – get away."

"Can you imagine how frustrating that would be for me," the Prince asked, "wondering what had happened to you and Gyõrgy and not being able to help if you were in any trouble?"

There was a sudden light in Forella's eyes as she asked,

"Would you – help me if I told you what was – wrong?"

"Shall I say," the Prince replied, "that I would try in every way in my power to do what is best for you."

He heard Forella give a little sigh of relief before she replied,

"I was afraid that you would be very – angry with me for taking Gyõrgy, but I could not believe that any horse could go – faster than he can."

"Is that why you chose him?"

"How could I resist anything quite so beautiful? And I was sure he could out-distance any other horse."

"How did you know that – ?" the Prince began.

Then he stopped.

"Listen, Miss Claye, we have to talk to each other. Will you have breakfast with me at one of my farms, which is not far from here?"

Forella hesitated.

He knew she was thinking that perhaps he was seeking an opportunity either to take the horse away from her so that she could not go any further or by some method to force her to return to The Castle with him.

"I am speaking without prejudice," he said, "and, as I have already promised that I will help you if I can, I hope you will trust me."

She looked at him and he thought that she had very strange eyes.

There was a touch of green in them, although it might well have been the reflection of the grass they were moving over.

"I – trust you," she said in a low voice after an obvious pause.

"Thank you," the Prince answered, "The farm is over there."

He pointed to where just in the distance there were some haystacks and, beyond them, smoke rising from a chimney.

As he spoke, he touched Jóska with his whip and, as the stallion swept forward, Gyõrgy followed.

As they rode at a fast pace towards the farm, the Prince thought he had never known a woman who could ride so well and who, in some magical way that he could not put a name to, could control a horse as wild as Gyõrgy without appearing to make any effort about it.

Only when they had reached the farm and the Prince had led the way to the stables did Gyõrgy protest.

He went through his usual routine of shying, rearing and bucking, but the Prince, who had already dismounted, watched Forella without interfering.

She not only kept in the saddle but controlled the horse in a manner that he himself could not have bettered and at the same time she was talking to him.

"Come on, boy, you are going to have a nice rest," she said. "I don't want you to be so tired by these gymnastics that you are too exhausted to take me – where I want to go."

There was something quiet and almost mesmeric about her voice, the Prince thought, for György, finding he could not unseat her, suddenly became docile.

He even allowed himself without any further objections to be taken into the stable and the stable door was closed behind him.

The Prince made no comment but walked to the farmhouse, where already waiting at the door was an apple-cheeked middle-aged woman who bobbed a curtsey as he reached her.

"Mornin', Your 'Ighness. It's nice to see you again. I were a-hopin' it wouldn't be long afore you came to see us."

"And so now I am here, Mrs. Hickson," the Prince replied, "and I have brought a young lady for breakfast who is as hungry as I am myself."

Mrs. Hickson curtseyed to Forella and led the way, talking nineteen to the dozen, into a comfortable parlour with a table in the window, which she quickly covered with a clean white cloth.

"You've come at the right time, Your Highness," she was saying. "Me husband killed a pig and I cured a ham only last week and I knows it'll be to your likin'."

"I am sure it will be," the Prince answered, "and I have always said, Mrs. Hickson, that nobody on the whole estate can cure a ham better than you."

With a smile of delight Mrs. Hickson hurried from the parlour and the Prince saw that Forella was standing on tiptoe, looking in the mirror over the mantelpiece as she removed her riding hat from her head.

When she turned round, he realised that he was looking at her properly for the first time and he could see how attractive she was. Yet her looks were unusual and different from those of anyone he had ever seen.

It was not only her hair with touches of gold in it and with little curls that had strayed from the *chignon* in which she had tried to keep them in place and which seemed to have a life of their own.

It was also that her eyes, which were very large, on either side of her small straight nose, had, as he had noticed in the field, a touch of green in them.

Her eyelashes were very long and, while they were dark at the roots, they curled upwards and the points were gold.

There was also something else that was strange about her, but for the moment he could not put a name to it.

She gave him a little smile that was one of shyness, then sat down at the table, saying as she did so,

"I admit, now that I think about it, to feeling — hungry."

The Prince sat down opposite her and said,

"We have much to talk about, but first it will make things easier if you will tell me your Christian name."

"Forella."

"And secondly how can you ride better than any woman I have ever seen?"

He paused before he added,

"I came looking for you, expecting to find an unconscious body with Gyõrgy careening away so that it would have taken hours, if not days, to catch him again."

"I have ridden since I was very young," Forella answered after a moment, "but of all the many horses I have ridden, I have never been on one quite as superlative as Gyõrgy."

There was silence.

Then she said impulsively,

"I-I would have sent him – back to you."

"I do not understand why you had to go away in the first place."

Then, as if the Prince was feeling for words, he added,

"Am I really such a bad host that you had to escape from The Castle so soon after your arrival?"

He spoke lightly, but to his surprise Forella looked out of the window and there was a note of desperation in her voice as she stammered,

"I-I have to – go!"

"Why?"

"I would – rather not tell you."

"I would greatly prefer to hear from you what has gone wrong rather than to hear it, as I undoubtedly shall, from your uncle and aunt on my return."

"I do *not* think they will – tell you the – truth."

"Then will you not tell me yourself what I should know?"

He was now aware that something was very wrong and he leant across the table, saying in a voice that every woman he had ever met found irresistibly beguiling,

"Please trust me, Forella. I swear that anything you tell me will be in confidence and I will do nothing to hurt you or to make things more difficult than they apparently are already."

Slowly, it seemed to him, she turned her head and raised her long eyelashes.

He was aware that she was looking deep beneath the surface as if she searched for some reassurance that she could trust him.

It was, the Prince thought, the first time in his life that any woman had looked at him in such a manner or was obviously debating within herself whether he was as trustworthy as he professed to be.

Then, as her strange eyes met his grey ones and they then looked at each other for a long moment, it seemed as if Forella was satisfied, because she said,

"There is nothing I can do – but run away and – hide."

"From what?"

"From what happened – last night."

"Will you tell me what happened?"

Forella drew in her breath, then after a moment she said in a voice he could barely hear,

"The Earl of – Sherburn came to my – bedroom by mistake – he thought it was – Lady Esme's room."

The Prince stiffened.

It was hard to believe that what he was hearing was the truth.

Then, as Forella went on, he understood.

"I-I was asleep," she said, "and, when I woke up, I was – frightened, because there was a – man in my room. Then before I could – say anything – Aunt Kathie came in."

The Prince did not need to hear any more.

He knew exactly what had happened and that this was the revenge Kathie Claydon had been planning when he saw the hatred in her eyes as she looked at Esme Meldrum across the drawing room.

It was a revenge that instinctively he had tried to prevent by flattering her and taking her to another room to see a painting he had bought.

But as Forella, a little incoherently, told him what had occurred, he could guess how it was that the Earl had mistaken, as Kathie had intended him to do, Forella's room for the one occupied by Esme.

And Kathie had been waiting like a cat at a mouse hole for him to do so.

"H-how can I – marry a man I have – never even spoken to?" Forella was asking. "That is why I had to – run away."

"I can understand your feelings," the Prince admitted very quietly.

"You – understand – you really do?"

"Of course I do," he replied. "But where were you going?"

She made a helpless little gesture which was somehow very pathetic.

"I have – only been in England for two weeks, but – I thought I could find somewhere where I could – hide from Aunt Kathie until it was – all forgotten."

"And you have some money with you?"

"I-I have a little."

"How much?"

"Nearly – five pounds."

"And you really think that would be enough to keep you from starvation?"

"I could – find something to do," Forella replied defensively.

"What can you do?"

"I have been thinking about that," she answered, "I can cook, although perhaps no one would employ me without a reference and I can also speak a number of languages including – Arabic."

The Prince was astonished.

"How can you do that?"

"I have travelled in a great many strange lands with my father."

"I am afraid I know nothing about you," the Prince said. "Please tell me, because I am curious about your father and mother, who I gather are now dead."

"My father died of typhoid in Naples at the end of February."

She thought that there was an expression of surprise on the Prince's face as if he was thinking it extraordinary that she was not in mourning and she explained quickly,

"Papa asked that no one should mourn for him because he did not – believe in death."

She paused before she added,

"In the East, where we had spent so much time, everyone believes in reincarnation. Papa believed that because he and Mama loved each other so much, they would both meet again in another life. He claimed that love is indestructible and cannot – die."

She spoke, the Prince now thought, without being in the least self-conscious about saying things that would make most women simper or feel embarrassed.

"So when your father died, you came back to England?"

"I would not have written to Uncle George," Forella said. "but our servant did. He had been with us ever since I was a child and he thought that it was the – right thing to do."

"Which, of course it was," the Prince approved.

"But I have no wish to live the sort of life that Papa always laughed at. He said Society was a lot of nonsense and consisted of foolish people who all competed with each other for bigger and better titles and wasted their time and energy in gambling, grumbling and gossip."

The way Forella spoke sounded so funny that the Prince could not help laughing.

"I think your father was right. At the same time there is not much alternative for young ladies like yourself."

"I have no wish to be a young lady," Forella said almost crossly. "I want to go on doing the things I did with Papa – only I am not quite certain how I can do them – alone."

"What sort of things did you do with your father?"

She gave him a mischievous little smile that told him he would be surprised at what she had to tell him.

"I was born in a – Bedouin tent," she answered. "And I have tried to find the source of the Ganges and have climbed the lower slopes of the Himalayas. I have encountered the Head Hunters in Sarawak and have dined with a tribe in Africa whose favourite dish was 'roast Christian'!"

The Prince stared at her incredulously and she laughed at the expression on his face.

It was a very natural sound, he thought, the spontaneous joyous laughter of a child.

"You did ask me," she said before he could speak, "but you do not have to believe me!"

"I think I would know if you were lying," the Prince answered.

"Why should you say that?"

"I have an instinct for such things and, although it seems incredible, I know that you are telling me the truth."

"Then, if you believe me, you will know that I have no wish to spend my life with people who are concerned mainly with how unkindly they can speak about one of their friends who is not present."

The Prince's lips twitched, but he replied,

"I think that is a rather cruel condemnation."

"Besides which," Forella carried on in a different tone, "I hate doing nothing but sitting all day in over-heated over-scented rooms, trying on clothes and eating at regular intervals."

She paused before she asked him,

"Have you any idea how much people like Uncle George and Aunt Kathie eat every day? If you put it all in a bucket, it would feed hundreds of – starving children in India."

She spoke almost passionately and the Prince said,

"I can understand that you are finding it all somewhat of a shock. Equally not everybody in the *Beau Monde* is quite as bad as you are making them out to be."

Forella gave a little shrug of her shoulders before she said,

"I have wanted to get away ever since I came to live in England and now I have to go! You must understand that."

"You don't think that marrying the Earl of Sherburn would give you a position in Society that most young women would think a very enviable one?" the Prince asked her.

"That is what Uncle George said to me and the answer is 'no!' How could I possibly marry a man if I did not love him? Anyway the Earl is in love – with someone else."

The Prince did not attempt to argue the point.

"The whole idea of being married just because Aunt Kathie wishes to be rid of me is so degrading and disgusting," Forella went on. "In any case I do not want a position in Society – or to be a puppet pulled by strings to say the right thing, do the right thing and think what I am told to think. I want to be free – I want to be myself!"

"And you are sure that it is quite impossible in the environment that your uncle and aunt live in?"

The Prince asked her the question very seriously and to his surprise, instead of glaring aggressively at him, Forella thought before she replied,

"That is the sort of question Papa and I used to discuss. I think that one can be oneself anywhere in the world, as long as one is not constrained into doing things which one knows –to be wrong."

There was silence for a moment before she went on,

"Papa said that all living is a search for the development of oneself and, because he and Mama were so blissfully happy, it did not matter what discomforts they might suffer, because they could laugh at them and every day was – one of discovery."

"What did they expect to find eventually?" the Prince asked.

"I suppose the real answer to that is their souls," Forella replied.

She spoke quite simply and the Prince thought it most unusual that anyone could say such things without seeming to be embarrassed about it.

Then before he could reply, the door opened and Mrs. Hickson came in carrying a tray loaded with food.

A little later Forella commented,

"Papa used to tell me how delicious English eggs and bacon were for breakfast. This is the first time – I have tasted them really fresh and I now know what he meant."

As she spoke, she helped herself to another piece of new bread warm from the oven and spread it with the golden butter that the Prince knew came from the herd of Jersey cattle that the Hicksons kept.

He poured himself out another cup of tea before he said,

"I think, Forella, we should now get back to the all-important question of what you are about to do."

"You have already agreed that I should go away," she said quickly.

"I said that I understand why you would wish to do so."

"But you will not stop me?"

"I suppose that is what I really should do," he replied.

She put down what she was eating and said in a very different tone,

"After bringing me here, you could not be so treacherous when I trusted you!"

"Which I hope you will continue to do," the Prince said. "At the same time you must see that what you are contemplating is quite impossible."

"I will make it possible and you have no right to interfere with me."

"I do not wish to do so, but I can appreciate better than you can the difficulties that lie ahead."

"I have overcome difficulties before."

"Not alone."

This was irrefutably true and she was silent as he went on,

"For a woman alone in the countryside there are dangers too many for me to enumerate and undoubtedly somebody would steal Györgi from you and you would find it hard without money and on your own to find any sort of accommodation."

"Why should I believe that?" Forella asked in a hostile voice.

"Because it is true in England," the Prince replied.

"Then the sooner I get out of this country the better!" Forella asserted. "Perhaps the best thing I could do would be to live abroad."

"What I am going to suggest is easier than that," the Prince said. "I do realise that you cannot turn to your father's relatives for assistance, but surely there must be some relatives of your mother's somewhere in the country?"

There was silence for a moment before Forella replied abruptly,

"My mother was not English."

To her surprise the Prince exclaimed,

"I was right! I felt there was something about you that was different. Now I know what it is and, unless I am very much mistaken, your mother was Hungarian!"

"Why should you say that?"

"Because no one could ride as well as you do if they did not have Hungarian blood in their veins and there is something about your face that has puzzled me, but now I know what it is."

"Yes, Mama was Hungarian," Forella admitted, "but Aunt Kathie said that I was to tell no one she was a foreigner because it was a disadvantage that might make men unwilling to marry me!"

The Prince put back his head and laughed.

"I have never heard of anything quite so ridiculous! And I suppose you know that I am Hungarian?"

"Yes, of course."

"Then why did you not tell me about your mother?"

"I did not think you would be – interested."

"But, of course, I am. What was her name before she married your father?"

"Rakozi, but I do not suppose you will have heard of them. Her family came from East Hungary."

"Of course I have heard of them," the Prince said. "They are a famous Hungarian family and, as it happens, their lands march with mine."

"Mama ran away with Papa, so if you are thinking of that, the Rakozis will certainly not welcome me!"

"I doubt if that is a fact," the Prince said. "At the same time it would take us too long a time to find out their feelings in the matter, so I have a very different suggestion to make."

"What is it?" Forella asked.

She spoke slowly and with a suspicious look in her eyes, which told him that she was afraid he was going to be difficult and somehow prevent her from escaping as she intended to do.

He seemed to be able in some strange way to read her thoughts and he knew that she was thinking that, if she could slip away when he was off his guard, she might take György from the stables and get away without his being aware of it.

He could almost see in the clearness of her eyes the thoughts going through her mind.

Then he said very quietly,

"We both have Hungarian blood in us, Forella, and even though I was prepared to help you before, I now consider I am honour-bound to do so, as a fellow countryman."

"You – you will help me?"

She was still not sure of him, but he thought that there was a flicker of light and hope in her eyes that had not been there before.

"I do realise," the Prince said slowly, "that it would be impossible for you, feeling as you do, to marry the Earl of Sherburn, even though from a Social point of view it would be a very brilliant if unexpected marriage."

"But – he is in love with Lady Esme," Forella said again.

The Prince secretly thought there was a more appropriate word for the feeling between the Earl and Esme Meldrum, but Forella, despite her wanderings all over the world, was too innocent to understand it.

"It would certainly be a very unhappy way for you to be married," he said, "and it is your feelings that matter to me. I am therefore going to suggest to you, Forella, an alternative to going off on your own in an unknown country and having to face dangers and privation, even the probability of starvation, with only five pounds in your pocket."

"If you are thinking of speaking to Aunt Kathie, I can tell you now she will not listen," Forella said quickly. "She wants to get me married so as to be rid of me and, I think, although I may be mistaken, that she also wants to punish the Earl in some way by making him take a – wife."

"Did you think that out for yourself?" the Prince enquired. "Or did somebody tell you that is what your aunt wanted to do?"

"I have been thinking it out since I saw the way she looked at me last night and heard the note in her voice," Forella replied. "I don't know why, but I am sure that she was angry with him not only because he was in my bedroom but for some other reason."

Now that the Prince had learnt that she was Hungarian, he knew that her instinct was as strong as his.

But there was no point in saying so now and he merely said,

"What I am going to suggest to you and I know that you will find it much safer and more comfortable than what you were contemplating is that you should instead hide in a house I own, which is about five miles across country from here."

"A house?" Forella asked.

"I have a relative of mine living in it," he replied. "Because she is partially crippled, she lives very quietly and alone in this house I gave her five years ago when she first came to England from Hungary."

"She is Hungarian?"

"As I said, she is one of my relatives."

"And – I could stay with her?"

"I think she would be delighted to have you. She does not speak English very well and in fact she knows nothing about the Social life in this country that you find so irksome. She is, however, a well-read, extremely intelligent person and I think you two would get on very well together."

Forella stared at him.

Then she asked,

"Are you really offering me sanctuary in your house? And you will not tell Uncle George or Aunt Kathie where I am hiding?"

"I will give you my word that I will not tell anybody where you are or that we have even met each other this morning. And when it is learnt at The Castle that you have disappeared, I shall pretend to be extremely surprised."

"What about the groom? He will tell them that I have taken Gyõrgy."

"Leave the groom to me," the Prince said. "I will think of some explanation, perhaps that Gyõrgy was found wandering in the fields and I left him in the care of one of my friends."

He smiled before he added,

"I expect you would like to be able to ride him while you are at Ledbury Manor."

"Is that the name of the house I would be going to?"

The Prince nodded.

Forella clasped her hands together.

"Can you really be so – kind and so – understanding?" she asked. "I don't know how to begin to thank you."

"As I have already said," the Prince replied, "a Hungarian calling to another Hungarian for help is something that is never ignored."

"Thank you – *thank you!*"

The Prince took his watch from his waistcoat pocket.

"As it will take us a little time to reach Ledbury Manor," he said, "I think we should start immediately. I must be back at The Castle for breakfast and then to face the music when your disappearance is reported."

There was a hint of mischief in Forella's eyes as she remarked,

"There is certainly one person who will be delighted at my disappearance and will hope I am conveniently dead and that is the Earl of Sherburn!"

The Prince laughed before he said,

"I am certainly not going to deny that. Osmond Sherburn has been saying for years that he has no intention of getting married."

"He will be glad and Aunt Kathie will be very angry!"

"My cousin will surely look after you very well," the Prince promised, "and incidentally her name is Princess Maria Dábas."

Forella gave him an enchanting smile as she said,

"It seems Fate, does it not, that Mama left home and everything that was Hungarian to be with Papa and so now I am going back to be saved by a Hungarian from what would most undoubtedly be hell for me."

"As you say," the Prince replied, "I think, Forella, Fate is playing a very decisive part in your life."

"But, of course," Forella said quietly, "and I shall believe in my Karma instead of being so frightened. I am now feeling rather ashamed of myself."

"I can only say it was understandable," he replied. "And now, come and show me once again how well you can handle György."

Without meaning to, as he rose from the table, he held out his hand to her as if she was a child.

As she slipped hers into it, he thought that from a Society point of view he was behaving very reprehensibly.

But his instinct and his Hungarian perceptiveness told him that not only was it right but there was actually no alternative.

CHAPTER FOUR

They had ridden for some way before the Prince informed her,

"I have been thinking about a new identity for you."

"Of course that is – important," Forella agreed.

"I think the best thing and certainly the most plausible," he said, "is to say that you are the daughter of a Hungarian friend who is coming to stay with me."

"Hungarian?" Forella interrupted.

"I am going to suggest that you take your mother's name," the Prince said, "and, unless I am mistaken, she had a title."

"She was a Countess," Forella confirmed, "but, of course, she never used it."

"Now it will come in useful. You will be the Countess Forella Rakozi."

Forella laughed.

"But I am trying to escape from Society and all its glittering baubles!"

The Prince smiled.

"On this occasion you must accept such frivolities. I suppose you can speak Hungarian well enough for people not to question your nationality?"

"You insult me!" Forella replied. "My mother usually spoke Hungarian when we were alone because she said that she wished to keep in practice and Papa spoke it so well, as he did many other languages, that

Mama said no one would believe that he was not a true Magyar!"

She spoke with a defiant note in her voice that the Prince had heard before and which he knew meant that she expected him to argue with her.

Instead he said almost humbly,

"I apologise."

"I think you are laughing at me," Forella said, "but I have so few possessions of my own that my intelligence is very precious to me."

It was such an original remark that the Prince laughed again.

He thought that his cousin, who as he had said was a very intelligent woman, would find Forella a relief in what was for the present a somewhat monotonous existence for her.

"Now we must straighten all this out in our minds," he suggested, "so that we both tell the same story."

He knew that Forella was listening intently as he went on,

"You set out a month or so ago from Hungary to come to England to stay with me, but when you reached Trieste, your father died there."

Forella realised that he was keeping as near as possible to the truth of what had actually happened.

"So you came to England alone," the Prince continued, "and, since you are in mourning, you have no wish to be in London, but you would rather stay quietly in the country, which is where I am taking you."

"It is a very good and convincing story," Forella cried, "and I will be extra careful to remember my new name."

"I am sure that will be no difficulty," the Prince replied, "and when we arrive I want you to write a note to your uncle."

"A note?"

The fear was back in Forella's eyes.

"Only to tell him that you have run away in order to stay with some friends," the Prince said quickly, "and that you are quite safe and that he has no need to worry over you."

She did not speak and after a moment he added,

"Otherwise, if you just disappear, there is every likelihood that your uncle will send the Police and certainly detectives in search of you."

Forella gave a cry of horror.

"That must not happen!"

"No, of course not," the Prince agreed. "Which is why it is important for you to write a note on which, naturally, there will be no return address."

"I think you are being very clever," Forella said, having thought it over, "and I am very – very grateful."

As she spoke, she thought that only a Hungarian could have entered into such a plot so competently and at the same time have understood that she could not go back and marry the Earl of Sherburn.

Then, since the Prince had very little time to spare if he was to get back to The Castle at a reasonable hour, he rode quickly and, as the horses galloped side by side, it was impossible to talk.

They had crossed the stream after leaving the farm and now Forella was well aware that the countryside they were riding through was, as she had expected, wilder and less inhabited than was the neighbourhood of The Castle.

There was only the occasional farmhouse to be seen in the distance and they rode for some way on what seemed entirely uninhabited land before the Prince said,

"This is Little Ledbury ahead of us."

For a moment Forella could see only trees and then a few thatched roofs amongst them.

As she rode on, she discovered a small village in which black-and-white cottages with their thatched roofs looked like something out of a Fairytale.

Each cottage had a little garden in front of it, brilliant with flowers and, except for a small bow-windowed shop looking onto the village green, there was little else in the village apart from the small Greystone Church.

As if she had asked the question, the Prince told her as they passed it,

"It was built in the seventeenth century and is one of the best examples of that period in England."

About fifty yards on from the Church they turned in through a gate with heraldic lions in stone on either side of it and, when Forella saw Ledbury Manor, she realised that it had been built at the same time as the Church.

Also of Greystone with pointed gables and high chimneypots, it was very beautiful and over the entrance there was a stone plaque commemorating its first owner with the date 1623 beneath it.

It was not very large, although it was built with three storeys and with diamond-paned windows and on one side of it was a high wall.

What made it especially dream-like was that perched on the roof and on the gables and fluttering round the courtyard were a large number of white doves.

They were so pretty that Forella gave an exclamation of delight and called out,

"Doves! The attendants of Aphrodite!"

However, the Prince did not answer and there was an expression on his face that she did not understand.

But there was no time to ask him questions.

As they dismounted, two grooms appeared, who saluted the Prince respectfully and led the horses away to the stables that could just be seen beyond some trees.

Gyõrgy attempted to play up, but he was obviously not so fresh after travelling at the fast speed set by Jóska and the groom soon quietened him.

However, Forella watched him anxiously and the Prince said to her,

"He will be all right. Thomas is a very experienced man or I would not have put him in charge of the stables here."

He made it sound as if there were quite a number of horses at The Manor and, as they then walked into the house, Forella wondered why, if his cousin was partly crippled, horses were of any great importance to her.

But she was feeling too apprehensive to ask any questions or to think of anything but her new identity.

The Prince, having greeted the butler, said to her,

"I am sure you would like to tidy yourself and it would be best for me to see my cousin alone before I introduce you."

"Yes, of course," Forella agreed at once.

The Prince turned to the butler,

"Newman, will you arrange for your wife to look after my guest?" he asked. "Then bring her down to the drawing room, where I expect I shall find Her 'Ighness."

"I'll see to it, Your'Ighness," Newman replied.

He led the way up the stairs and, by the time they reached the top, an elderly woman was waiting for them. She gave Forella a respectful little curtsey and said,

"Welcome, ma'am, it's very pleasin' for us to see His 'Ighness here again."

She did not wait for Forella to answer her, but led the way into a very attractive bedroom with flowered chintz curtains.

The windows looked out over a beautifully kept garden that Forella could see led down to a small stream.

Mrs. Newman was talking all the time she was helping Forella to take off her riding hat and then the jacket of her habit.

"It's very hot, ma'am," she said, "and Her 'Ighness'll understand that you'll feel more comfortable in your blouse."

It was in fact a very pretty blouse, which the Marchioness had bought and which Forella thought at the time had been exceedingly expensive.

Of white lawn and inset with real lace, the shop assistant had assured her that it had just come from Paris, as had the habit, which was very French, being made of green pique edged with white braid.

"It is something you certainly could not follow the hounds wearing," the Marchioness had exclaimed. "At the same time women who want to go riding in the summer are allowed to deck themselves out like peacocks and you will certainly attract attention if nothing else."

Because she had been far too busy in simply making her escape to think about clothes, it was only now that Forella remembered that she had only one gown in the roll that she had attached to György's saddle.

However, she thought it was best not to mention what she had brought with her until she knew that the Prince's cousin would have her to stay.

She therefore washed her face and hands and Mrs. Newman tidied her hair.

Then, feeling a little self-conscious, she walked to the top of the stairs, to see Newman waiting for her in the hall.

Only as she went down towards him did she pray that there would be no slip-up in the Prince's plans at the last moment, so that after all she would have to set out on her own.

Now that she thought about it, she realised just how frightening it would be by herself.

When she had run away in sheer panic, she had not had any time to think out the details or even to decide how she would manage with György and only a very little money between her and starvation.

'The Prince is right and he is very – very – kind,' she thought as she reached the hall.

Then she wondered with a sudden fear that, if by the time that she reached him, he might have changed his mind.

But, as she was shown into the low-ceilinged attractive drawing room with the sunshine coming through the casement windows in a golden flood, she knew as he rose to his feet that all was well.

As if he was aware of what she was feeling, he crossed to her side and, taking her hand, said,

"Cousin Maria, this is Forella Rakozi, whom I have been telling you about."

He spoke in Hungarian and the Princess held out her hand and, as she did so, she said in the same language, "You poor child, I am so sorry for you and, of course, you can stay here with me for as long as you wish. It will be delightful for me to have somebody who can speak my own language."

Forella curtseyed and said,

"It is very gracious of Your Highness."

As she looked at the Princess, she saw that she had once been very beautiful and still in her old age had a distinction that obviously came from her personality and character.

Instinctively Forella was drawn to her and she was almost sure that the Princess felt the same.

Then, as she sat down, the Princess said,

"You are very lovely, and it is not surprising for the Rakozis are noted for their beautiful women, are they not, János?"

"So I have always heard," he replied, "and so I am certainly ready to agree with what you say."

"You flatter me," Forella said, but her eyes were twinkling in a way that told the Prince that she was amused by his play-acting.

"I am afraid you may find it very dull here," the Princess said to her, "but János tells me you are in mourning and that you wish to be very quiet."

"That is what I hope to find," Forella answered, "and I can only thank you for having me as your guest."

"I should be thanking you," the Princess replied. "But I cannot pretend that the place is a whirl of gaiety."

She looked rather reproachfully at the Prince as she spoke, but he laughed.

"You are trying to make me feel sorry for you, Cousin Maria," he protested, "but you know as well as I do that your Doctors have told you to rest and, apart from other reasons, for the moment at any rate this is the right place for you to be."

As if she felt he was reproaching her, the Princess put her hand on his arm and said,

"I am not really grumbling, János, and you know I can never thank you sufficiently for all you have done for me."

"Now you are making me embarrassed," the Prince asserted, "and I am going to leave Forella with you while I return to look after my house party."

"Is it then the usual collection of pleasure-seeking beautiful women and women-seeking handsome men?" the Princess enquired.

The Prince laughed.

"I could not describe it more accurately myself!"

He kissed her hand.

Then he said,

"Forgive me if I take Forella with me for just a moment into the morning room. She has some addresses to give me of people I have to contact on her behalf."

"Yes, of course," the Princess replied, "and I am sure you will find everything you want. If not Newman will be able to provide it."

Forella rose to her feet as the Princess added,

"When shall we see you again?"

"Quite soon," the Prince answered. "Perhaps before I return to London when the party is over."

"I shall be delighted to see you again," the Princess replied.

She sat back in her chair to watch Forella walk with the Prince towards the door.

Then she picked up the newspaper she had been reading before she had been interrupted and carefully studied the *Court Circular* for her cousin's name.

*

The Prince and Forella went into the morning room and, when he had closed the door, he said,

"Write the letter to your uncle and I also require you to give me your measurements."

"My measurements?" Forella exclaimed in surprise.

"I cannot believe you expect to wear what you have on day after day without a change," he replied, "and for once I imagine it to be true when a woman says that she has 'nothing to wear'!"

"I had really forgotten about clothes," Forella said, "and I suppose the Princess will think it strange if I do not have any."

"Very strange," the Prince answered. "I must therefore send for some from London."

There was a long pause in the conversation and a faint colour came into Forella's cheeks as she responded uncomfortably,

"I feel it – is an – imposition."

"So what you are really saying," the Prince said, "is that it is highly unconventional, but everything you are doing and have done so far, Forella, has been *very* unconventional and it is no use straining at a gnat and swallowing a camel!"

Forella gave a little chuckle and he knew that she was thinking about the camels she had ridden and how unpredictable and usually bad-tempered such animals were.

It was odd, he thought once again, how he could read her thoughts and he liked the way she replied,

"You are helping me because you are Hungarian. Perhaps one day, as a Hungarian, I will be able to help you."

"Shall I say that I do not look on it as a debt," the Prince said, "but as a responsibility of mine simply because the unfortunate circumstances in which you find yourself happened in my house."

"The person who put me into such a mess is the Earl of Sherburn," Forella flashed, "and it should actually be his responsibility and not yours."

The Prince smiled and said,

"I think, however, you are not prepared to point out to him what is his duty."

Forella gave a little cry that was half-serious and half-joking.

"I will write the note," she said, "and will pray as I do so that Uncle George will believe I am all right and will not send detectives searching for me."

There was a writing desk in the window and so she sat down and took a piece of writing paper from a leather holder, which she noticed bore the Prince's insignia.

Then she found lying beside the blotter a pair of jewelled scissors to cut off the address from the top of the writing paper.

Carefully she wrote what the Prince had told her to,

"Dear Uncle George,

I have gone away because it is impossible for me to marry the Earl of Sherburn when he has no wish to marry me.

The only thing I can do is to disappear so that

nobody will know what has happened and it will be easy for them to forget I ever existed. I am staying with friends and am quite safe, so please do not worry about me or try to find me.

Thank you for all your kindnesses that I am very grateful for.

I remain your affectionate niece,
Forella."

Once she had written the note, she read it through to see that there were no mistakes before she held it out to the Prince, who was standing with his back to the fireplace.

He took it from her and then handed it back, saying,

"Very good. But be careful to put it into an envelope without a crest on the back."

Forella found one in the blotter, put the note inside it and sealed it down. Then she wrote on another piece of paper her measurements, which, after her many fittings in London, she knew exactly.

She rose from the writing desk and handed both the note and the paper to the Prince as she said,

"I am afraid I have nothing with me except one dress and a nightgown, but please do not spend too much money or it will take me a very long time to pay you back."

"I thought I had already made it clear that what I send you is a gift," the Prince said, "but I am wondering now whether you would prefer to be dressed as an English *debutante* or as a Hungarian."

"There is no need for me to answer that," Forella said with a smile. "All the same I was very happy in the clothes that I wore with Papa, which Aunt Kathie said were fit only for the dustbin, which was where she put them."

"I understand exactly what you are trying to say to me," the Prince replied, "but I have always believed that a beautiful picture deserves a beautiful frame."

"Now you are talking like an actor in a play," Forella said. "I thought last night when I was at The Castle that the whole thing was not real – but was taking place on a stage!"

She thought that he looked a little surprised and went on,

"It amused the audience, but they did not believe for a single moment that the actors and actresses were real or projecting anything that actually came from their hearts."

The Prince realised incredulously that she was mocking him and he replied,

"I am just wondering, Forella, why you should set yourself up as a critic, judge and jury, and on whose authority you consider yourself justified in putting forward such preposterous suppositions."

For a moment there was silence.

Then Forella said humbly,

"You are – quite right, Your Highness. I am being – impertinent and – I am sorry. I forgot for the – moment that I was not – speaking to Papa. We used to duel with each other in words and always tried to – score points off each other."

She blushed and the Prince felt that he had not only been cruel but unsportsmanlike to one so young and vulnerable and, as he was now aware, very sensitive.

"I like duelling, as you call it, with you," he said quickly, "and it is something I have not done in the same way with anyone else."

He felt that she was not appeased and so added,

"I do want you to go on being frank with me and saying what you think. I do not believe that the Social world I live in is as depraved as you make out, but I have to acknowledge that there is a modicum of truth in what you say."

She did not reply and he realised he had driven the smile from her lips and the mischief from her eyes and asked himself how he could have been so clumsy.

At the same time he was even more aware than he had been before that she could never cope with the world on her own.

When he said 'goodbye', Forella thanked him again and her gratitude was very sincere.

As she stood on the steps and watched him mount Jóska, who had been brought from the stables, the Prince felt that she looked very young and very much alone.

As he rode on, he hoped that he had done the right thing in helping her as she had asked him to do.

But he was aware that he had taken a heavy responsibility upon himself and had behaved in a manner that most people would think extremely reprehensible.

After all in the Social world no young girl could ask more than to be the wife of the Earl of Sherburn, whatever the circumstances that obliged him to make her his bride.

The Prince knew that in England, as in most countries, the daughters of aristocrats had no choice over who they married.

In fact marriage involved exactly the same sort of bargaining contract that had begun in Roman times, which meant a business exchange of money or land.

It was assumed that just as Royalty married Royalty, so aristocrat should marry aristocrat and blue blood marry blue blood.

Despite the fact that Kathie had tricked Osmond Sherburn into marrying her niece, the Prince knew that the Marquis would ultimately think it was an excellent match from Forella's point of view and from his own.

'I suppose if I thought like an Englishman and did what an Englishman does,' the Prince told himself, 'I would either have made Forella come back with me to The Castle or would now behave in what she would consider a treacherous manner and tell Claydon where she is.'

But he was not English, he was Hungarian and, having given Forella his word, he would not break it.

'Besides,' he tried to appease his conscience, 'she is so very different from the ordinary English *debutante*, which, of course, is because she is half-Hungarian.'

He arrived back at The Castle before nine o'clock, at which time he knew the gentlemen in the house party would be gradually staggering downstairs for breakfast.

The ladies would then ring much later for their maids, the majority of them not appearing before luncheontime.

It was therefore quite easy for the Prince, as he walked towards his bedroom, to leave the note Forella had written for her uncle on a table in the corridor outside her room.

He thought it was unlikely that it would be found and taken to the Marquis until much later and he would have told Barton that he had seen no sign of György or the horse's rider and had therefore returned to The Castle, hoping that they had come back by another route.

Having seen Barton, he wrote to a dressmaker in Bond Street who he had spent large sums of money with in the past.

He went to the library, where, as he expected, most of his male guests were congregated and reading the newspapers.

Amongst them was the Marquis, who bade him 'good morning' in a quite ordinary tone of voice.

The Prince thought with some satisfaction that he and his wife must have arranged for 'the fireworks' to be let off later on.

There was no sign of the Earl and it was an hour or so later when the Prince learnt that he had gone out riding accompanied by Lady Esme.

One of the reasons why the Prince's parties were always such a success was that he made it clear that his guests could do exactly as they wished and so every facility was provided for their amusement.

There were horses and carriages available for them to ride or drive, there were boats on the lake, two Croquet greens, several tennis courts and he had recently installed a covered court, which was a delight when it was raining.

There was also a golf course and inside The Castle the inevitable billiard room.

As the Prince then thought of the Earl and Lady Esme, he found himself anticipating what their conversation would be and thought that later on in the day the Earl was in for a pleasant surprise.

*

As they rode slowly through the woods where the rides had been cut wide enough for two horses to move side by side, the Earl was saying,

"What am I to do, Esme? What the hell am I to do about it?"

"I think it is disgraceful of Kathie to behave in such an underhand manner," Lady Esme exclaimed, "that I feel l can never speak to her again."

She was looking exquisitely beautiful, at the same time a little pale due to the fact that she had lain awake for half the night wondering why the Earl had not come to her as he had promised he would.

When she had received a note from him soon after she was called, she had known even before she read it that something was very wrong.

"I must see you immediately and I suggest we go riding.

I will be waiting in the stables in half-an-hour's time."

It was difficult for Esme to dress so quickly, even with the help of her very experienced lady's maid, but somehow she managed it.

When she joined the Earl and raised her blue eyes reproachfully to his, she was then astounded by the expression on his face.

Although it seemed impossible, he appeared to have aged considerably since she had last seen him and there was a grimness about the tightness of his lips and the darkness of his eyes which she did not understand.

Only when he had told her what had occurred did she give a cry of anger and frustration that made him want to hold her in his arms and comfort her.

"It is diabolical! *Absolutely diabolical!* Kathie is a devil to plan anything quite so cruel and wicked."

"It is my fault," the Earl said. "We should not have used the Prince of Wales's signal, which has been laughed about in every Club and I suspect in every boudoir."

"There were no white roses in the vase in my room," Esme explained, "so I put a lily outside the door instead."

It flashed through the Earl's mind that the choice of flower would have made Kathie sneer and perhaps made her feel even angrier than before.

He was aware that, while Kathie had taken a number of lovers since she had begun to be unfaithful to her husband, he would have been Esme's first and therefore the lily was in some ways appropriate.

"If only I could have come to you, darling, last night after it had happened and told you all about it," he said, "it would have been better than having to go to my own room and be alone with all the demons of Hell taunting me for being caught in a trap."

"That is exactly what it was," Esme exclaimed indignantly, "a trap set by Kathie! I hate her, Osmond, do you hear me? *I hate her!*"

"I feel very much the same way," the Earl admitted. "The question is, how can I prevent myself from being marched up the aisle to marry her niece when all I want is to remain a single man?"

As he finished speaking, he thought that it sounded rather impolite and so added quickly,

"And to be with you, my lovely one."

"That is exactly what I want," Esme said softly, "but after all, Osmond darling, if you are married, as I am married, it would not really make very much difference."

*

It was not until nearly luncheontime that the Marchioness, putting the finishing touches to her appearance, said to her maid,

"Jones, go and tell Miss Forella I wish to speak to her and, if she has gone downstairs already, tell one of the servants to find her for me."

"Very good, my Lady," Jones said, "but, as I haven't heard her movin', I expects she's still asleep."

"Then wake her up," the Marchioness said sharply.

However, she was smiling as she looked at her reflection in the mirror.

She had certainly made the Earl pay for his treatment of her.

She had also made quite certain this morning before George went down to breakfast that he would not go back on his decision that the Earl must marry Forella.

"It was damned careless of him, if you were to ask me, for Sherburn to go bursting into the wrong room," the Marquis had said. "At the same time this place is like a rabbit warren."

"As you say, George," his wife replied, "it was extremely careless. But, whatever the reason, it would be a great mistake for poor little Forella to suffer."

She took a quick glance at her husband to see if he was listening and went on,

"You know as well as I do that if there was the slightest whisper about his going to her bedroom let alone being seen leaving it, the child would be ostracised by all the important London hostesses."

She paused to add impressively,

"We could never, never, by any possible means, find her a husband who would overlook such a thing!"

"All right, Kathie, I know what you are saying," the Marquis answered irritably. "At the same time, I like Osmond and I feel it is really caddish to throw him such a backhander."

"Whatever you may or might not think, George," the Marchioness replied, "it is some satisfaction to know that with Osmond's fortune you will have no need to give Forella any dowry. He can well afford to look after his wife."

"I was not thinking about money," the Marquis retorted. "I am thinking about Sherburn, and, of course, Forella. She will be no more able to cope with him than a babe in arms!"

He did not wait for his wife's reply, but went out of the room, closing the door behind him unnecessarily loudly.

The Marchioness was not perturbed. She merely gave a low laugh and then thought that by now the Earl would be really regretting that he had ever left her.

Jones, having knocked on the door of Forella's bedroom and received no answer, had entered it quietly.

The sunshine was coming through the uncurtained windows and one glance told her that Forella was not there.

She therefore went to the top of the stairs and, having beckoned one of the footmen on duty in the hall to come up to her, asked him to go and find Miss Forella.

"I hears the maid who looks after her say," he answered, "that she's gone off ridin' and hasn't come back."

"Well, she should be back soon," Jones retorted. "Tell her when she does appear that her Ladyship wants her."

The footman grinned and scuttled back to the hall as Jones returned to the Marchioness.

"I've made enquiries, my Lady," she said, "and it appears Miss Forella's out a-ridin'."

The Marchioness glanced at the clock,

"She will be very late for luncheon. Really, how tiresome these girls are! An empty place at the table will certainly annoy the Prince."

"There's time yet, my Lady, for Miss Forella to come back and change," Jones said.

By this time, although the Marchioness was not yet aware of it, a housemaid dusting the corridor had found the note addressed by Forella to her uncle.

She took it down the backstairs to the pantry, where the footman who took it from her waited for the butler, who had gone down to the cellar to return before he handed it to him.

The butler put on his tailcoat to find a silver salver before, without hurrying, he carried the note through the house to the library where he knew that the Marquis was likely to be.

By now the guests were beginning to assemble for luncheon and just before the butler brought in the note, first the Earl and then a little later Esme Meldrum joined the others.

"You are very energetic, Sherburn," somebody remarked to the Earl. "I had intended to go riding this morning, but what with the late hour we went to bed and I suspect our host's excellent wine, the effort proved too much for me."

The Earl murmured a somewhat incoherent reply and then hid himself behind a copy of *The Times*.

As he appeared to be somewhat out of sorts, he was left alone.

When Esme appeared, the Marchioness said with a false smile,

"How fresh you look. It must be the effect of riding so energetically and so early."

"It was very enjoyable," Lady Esme managed to say in an affected voice, hoping that her hatred for the Marchioness did not show in her blue eyes.

Then she crossed over the room to talk to two other women who had found it far more agreeable to lie in bed than to face the sunshine.

The butler stopped beside the Marquis and held out the note on the silver salver.

The Marquis took it, wondering why he should receive a letter when he had given strict instructions to his servants in Park Lane that, as he was to be away only for the weekend, he did not wish anything forwarded.

He pulled Forella's note out of the envelope, read it, then expostulated almost beneath his breath,

"Good God!"

He read it again to be quite certain he had not made a mistake, then walked to where his wife was talking animatedly to the Prince and drew her on one side.

"What is it, George?" she asked, thinking it was most inconsiderate of him to interrupt at such a moment.

"I have something to show you," the Marquis said quietly.

He took her arm in a determined manner and drew her to a corner of the room where they could not be overheard.

Because there was nothing she could do about it, she went with him with an ill grace.

Only when he had handed her Forella's note and she had read it did she stare at the paper as if she could not believe her eyes.

"I thought she had no friends in England," she remarked at length.

"If she has, I have no idea who they are."

"Then what are you going to do?"

"What can we do?" the Marquis enquired.

The Marchioness folded the note and put it back into the envelope.

Then she threatened,

"If this is a plot between her and Osmond Sherburn, I will kill him!"

"You cannot make a scene here," the Marquis said quickly.

"No, of course not," his wife replied, "but I will speak to Osmond after luncheon."

There was no time now for at that moment the butler went up to Lady Roehampton and announced,

"Luncheon is served, my Lady."

Lady Roehampton, who had been then talking to the Prince at the other end of the room, began to collect the ladies to move into the dining room.

Only as she reached the Marchioness did she say, as she was the most important woman present,

"Go ahead, Kathie dear."

"I am afraid, although you will think it very bad manners," the Marchioness said, "that Forella will not be here for luncheon. I can only say how sorry I am for not letting you know sooner, but I will explain afterwards."

Lady Roehampton, without any comment, gave instructions to the butler to remove one place from the table.

As they walked towards the dining room, she was wondering how she could rearrange the table so that two men would not be sitting together.

She soon decided it would be impossible, but managed instead very skilfully to seat side by side two sportsmen who had a common interest in racing. This meant that they had plenty to discuss and did not mind that there was no female between them.

Watching the Earl the Marchioness thought he looked round the table apprehensively as if he was searching for Forella.

She was quite certain that it was just a pretence and he was well aware that she had left.

'He has persuaded her to go away so that he can somehow get out of the engagement,' she calculated, 'but it is something I will never let him do. He will marry her even if George has to challenge him to a duel to make him do so!'

She was quite certain it would not come to that, because both the Earl and the Marquis had a horror of scandal or of being written about in a derogatory way in the newspapers.

The Marchioness thought that she would enjoy every moment of the marriage in which the Earl was the reluctant bridegroom and humiliated by knowing she had the upper hand!

Whatever happened in the future, he would always know that she was laughing at him.

'I have won! *I have won*!' she told herself triumphantly. 'He will regret that he left me every time he looks at the woman who bears his name!'

As the ladies then left the dining room after luncheon was finished, she managed, as she passed the Earl, to say in a voice that only he could hear,

"I must see you, Osmond, it is important."

She thought he was about to refuse her, but when the gentlemen came into the library a little later, she moved to his side and suggested,

"Let us go into the garden. I have something to show you."

She knew that he was longing to walk away from her and not have to listen to what she had to say.

But, presumably feeling that it might make things even worse than they were already, he acquiesced with a bad grace.

As she knew him so well, she was aware of what he was feeling without having to look at the squareness of his chin and the hardness of his eyes.

They walked across the lawn until they were out of earshot of any of the others who had come out onto the terrace.

Without saying anything, the Marchioness handed him Forella's note.

She waited until he had read it and then she said,

"As this is your doing, I wish to know where you have sent her."

"It has nothing at all to do with me and I have no idea where the girl has gone," the Earl replied sharply.

"Do you really expect me to believe that?"

"You may believe what you like," he retorted. "I can only imagine she had the good taste to be disgusted by your behaviour last night and too shy for either your company or mine."

"You are very eloquent," the Marchioness sneered, "but, as you can imagine, George is very perturbed as to what has happened to Forella. She has never been to England before. She has no friends and from all I can gather from the servants, she went riding before breakfast on one of the Prince's horses and has not returned."

For the first time the Earl seemed interested.

"She went alone?"

"*Of course* she went alone," the Marchioness snapped. "She knows nobody in the house except for her uncle and me."

The Earl put Forella's note back into the envelope.

"Well, all I can say is that she shows a great deal of good sense."

"Do not talk like that," the Marchioness said angrily. "Tell me where she has gone."

"I can only repeat that I have absolutely no idea," the Earl answered her, "and I know nothing about your niece. Except that, as I have already said, I think she has shown a great deal of common sense."

"Are you telling me that is all you have to say in the matter?" the Marchioness queried.

"What do you expect me to say?" he replied. "Do you want me to call out the hounds and hunt her down as if she was a fox?"

He paused to say slowly,

"As far as I am concerned, she can stay away as long as she likes, because, Kathie, one thing is certain, until you can produce her, it would be quite useless and would cause a great deal of comment if you announced our engagement."

There was an expression of satisfaction on the Earl's face that made the Marchioness long to strike him.

Then, because she had no answer to what he had said and, because she knew it was the truth, she walked away from him, her bustle moving as she did so like a tempestuous sea!

CHAPTER FIVE

As Forella dismounted from Gyõrgy at the front door of the house, she said to Thomas, who had escorted her on her ride,

"Thank you very much, that was very enjoyable."

"I enjoyed it too, my Lady," Thomas replied.

As he rode off to the stables, he took off his cap and Forella, walking into the house, thought what a nice man he was.

When she wished to go riding on Gyõrgy and was aware that she must be accompanied by a groom, she had been afraid that he would slow the pace and complain if she rode too far ahead of him.

But to her considerable surprise she found that the stables of The Manor contained a dozen exceptionally fine horses and that Thomas, who was in charge of them, was different from how she expected an ordinary English groom to be.

A good-looking man of about forty, he was, she thought, better mannered and certainly far better educated than seemed appropriate to his position in life.

Of course she had had no experience of any English stables, but at least she knew when a man was an expert with horses and there was no doubt that it was what Thomas was.

If she appreciated him, she realised from the first moment after they had ridden together that he appreciated her.

It would have been impossible for anyone seeing the way she handled Gyõrgy, who was usually extremely obstreperous when she first mounted him, not to be aware that she could ride any animal, however wild.

When Gyõrgy was more or less under control, Thomas said,

"I congratulate you, my Lady."

Forella flashed him a smile.

"It is only Gyõrgy's fun," she said, "and I have never enjoyed riding a horse so much or looked forward to riding as much as I am this morning."

"I feel sure you will not be disappointed," Thomas said.

He took her for miles and, as it was in the opposite direction from where she knew that The Castle was situated, she was not afraid of seeing any members of the house party.

Actually they saw very few people, only some men working in the fields and sometimes a farmer's gig trundling along the narrow lanes.

It was two days later when Forella plucked up enough courage to ask,

"Why does His Highness want so many horses here? And who is there to ride them?"

There was a little pause before Thomas replied,

"Some of them are carriage horses, my Lady, and the others His Highness leaves with me so that I can break them in when he has not the time to do it himself."

"You have worked for him for long?" Forella enquired.

Again there was a little pause before Thomas replied,

"I have in fact been with His Highness for nearly three years."

It was obvious that Thomas did not wish to be communicative and she thought it was an intrusion to ask him too many questions.

Equally she was very curious about him and increasingly so, as the days passed, about a number of other things.

She could not understand the organisation of The Manor itself, which she had thought so beautiful when she had first arrived.

Mrs. Newman brought breakfast to her in her bedroom, suggesting that, as the Princess always had breakfast in bed, she would be more comfortable upstairs than sitting alone in the dining room.

"It will be very luxurious," Forella had answered.

As she spoke, she was thinking that in the last few years since her mother's death, she had usually risen early to prepare her father's breakfast. Even when they had servants they did not always give him the food he liked.

At other times when they were travelling, breakfast had often been cooked over a camp fire or consisted of a native meal of maize and nuts made more palatable with coconut milk.

. But whatever it was, even if it was fresh from a tree, Forella always brought it to her father and waited for him to tell her if it was to his liking.

Sometimes, almost as if he was homesick, he would say,

"I am so fed up with this food. I want a good English breakfast of eggs and bacon and a choice from a half-a-dozen silver dishes laid out on a side table as there used to be at home."

Then he would laugh and add,

"I must be growing senile if that is the sort of life I would want. But it is doubtless what will happen to me in my old age."

Then he would start to talk excitedly of some new country that he wanted to explore or an expedition that required a great deal of planning and invariably cost more than they could afford.

The second morning after she had finished her breakfast, Forella heard a soft cooing note at the open window and saw one of the white doves sitting on the ledge, regarding her with a curious eye.

She got out of bed slowly and carefully so as not to frighten it away and, taking a piece of toast from the silver rack, she walked across the room, breaking it into small pieces as she did so.

The dove, however, was not in the least frightened and waited for her to place a small piece of toast in front of him, which he ate. Then he took the rest from the palm of her hand.

As he flew away, Mrs. Newman came into the room.

"You've finished your breakfast, my Lady?" she enquired.

"Yes, thank you," Forella replied, "and what I could not eat, one of those lovely white doves gobbled it down as if he was not too fat already."

She laughed, but there was a frown between Mrs. Newman's eyes.

"I don't think you should feed them here, my Lady," she said. "They belong to the 'Poor Lady'."

"The 'Poor Lady'?" Forella questioned.

Mrs. Newman turned away and picked up the tray.

"No, I'm sure it's all right," she said quickly. "Please forget what I said just now, my Lady. I made a mistake."

She went from the room before Forella could say anything more. But she stared after her, thinking it very strange that she was so abrupt and wondering who the 'Poor Lady' could be.

She supposed she was referring to the Princess, but so far she had not seen her feeding the doves.

In fact Forella remembered that only yesterday she had complained about them, saying they made so much noise that they woke her up in the morning and there were really getting to be too many of them.

"But they are so pretty," Forella had expostulated.

"They may be, but they do make a mess," the Princess had replied and then had started to talk about something else.

But if it was not the Princess, who was the 'Poor Lady'?

Forella had found that there were quite a number of servants in the house, many more than she would have expected.

She was very ignorant of how English houses were run, although her father had told her of the army of servants that his father and her grandfather had employed in their ancestral home in Huntingdonshire.

She could remember how he used to enumerate them for her, starting with the scullery boy and ending with the Groom-of-the-Chambers, who he said was so important that the staffs were as frightened of him as they were of their Master.

Because he enjoyed talking about his home and his ancestors, Forella would beg him to tell her more and more about it.

He would then describe to her in every detail how he had been brought up when he was a small boy and the big parties which had been given at Claye Park.

When she was alone with her mother, she would also encourage her to talk of her life in Hungary, the Palace where her family lived and the acres of land they owned in the East of Hungary.

It had been a fascinating contrast, which she had stored in her memory.

Ever since coming to England she had wished over and over again that her father was with her to make her laugh at all the rules and regulations which he had dispensed with in his life.

But she knew that it was what made a house as big as the Prince's Castle run as smoothly as clockwork.

The Manor was very small in contrast and yet there were mob-capped maids in gingham dresses who cleaned the house in the morning and young footmen with crested buttons on their Livery who helped Newman to wait on the Princess at mealtimes.

Forella often wondered what they did when they had finished in the dining room, but she suspected that Newman, who had plenty of authority about him, kept them busy one way or another.

As far as she was concerned, every day was an enchantment that she had not expected to find.

There was always the joy of riding immediately after breakfast when the Princess had no wish for her company.

In the afternoon she found herself enjoying every moment of the Princess's conversation, which was clever, informative and at the same time so human and understanding that Forella felt almost as if she was listening to somebody reading her Fairy stories.

It was on Tuesday, when both she and the Princess were hoping that the house party would have broken up and the Prince would call and see them, that the Princess said,

"Did János tell you about me?"

"He said you were his cousin and that he had given you this house when you came to England."

"He did not say why I had to come here?"

"No."

"Then you might as well know that if there is an Archangel on this earth, then it is János Kovác!"

"I had not thought of him quite like that, although he has been very very kind to me," Forella said.

"He is kind to everybody," the Princess said with a smile. "There is nobody who has ever turned to János for help who has not received it and I lie awake at night wondering why such a man with so much goodness in his heart should not be happy."

"He is not happy?" Forella asked in surprise.

She thought that the Princess was about to say something, but then suddenly changed her mind to say instead,

"The rich are not always as happy as people imagine them to be."

"Tell me in what way the Prince has been kind to you," Forella asked.

The Princess paused for a moment.

Then she said,

"There is no reason why you should not know. As he told you, I am his cousin, but from a different generation. I suppose like all Hungarian families the Kovács stick together through thick and thin, except when one of us, as I did, deliberately severs the ties that bind us to one another."

Forella was becoming interested.

"What do you mean?" she asked.

The Princess smiled as she said,

"I married the man I loved!"

"And the Kovács did not approve?"

"They disapproved violently, eloquently and furiously."

"But, why?"

"That is what I will now tell you, my dear," the Princess said. "My husband was not an aristocrat, not quite a 'man of the people', but very nearly and he was also a revolutionary."

"How exciting!"

Forella looked at the Princess with widening eyes and, as if she enjoyed having such an attentive audience, the old lady went on,

"When they threatened to shoot Imbe Dabás if he came near me, I ran away with him."

"How brave of you!"

As Forella spoke, she thought that perhaps it was easier to run away with somebody one loved rather than alone as she had tried to do.

"I crept out at night just like a character in a romantic novelette," the Princess went on, "carrying everything valuable I possessed wrapped up in a shawl. Imbe was waiting for me and we rode off away from my father's Palace, knowing that if we were caught Imbe would undoubtedly die and I should be more or less imprisoned in The Palace with no chance of ever escaping."

"But you got away!" Forella exclaimed.

"We rode for two days without sleep," the Princess said, "until we were off my father's land. Then we were married."

"Where was that?"

"In a little Church at the foot of the mountains."

"And you never regretted running away?"

"Never, *never!*" the Princess cried. "I loved Imbe and he adored me. I suppose you could say that that we were made for each other and we were only complete as one person when we were together."

"It sounds very romantic!" Forella said. "And it is what my father and mother felt about each other."

"That is real love and whatever happened in the future, I knew from the moment Imbe made me his wife that I was the luckiest woman in the whole world."

Her voice as she spoke was very moving and Forella enquired,

"What happened after that?"

"We went on living in Hungary," she said, "but Imbe became notorious as a man who was always attacking the complacency of the Government, asking for reforms and taking up the causes of those who were downtrodden and unjustly treated."

"Did you help him?" Forella asked.

"I helped him by loving him and by keeping his home life completely separate from his public one."

Forella must have looked a little disappointed for the Princess added,

"It was what he wanted. As I was so precious to him, he would not allow me to expose myself to a world where he was constantly abused and consistently misunderstood."

"1 suppose that happens to all reformers," Forella murmured.

"You are right," the Princess said, "and yet, while a great many people decried Imbe and hated him, he did get a great many abuses reformed, which would never have happened if he had not fought for those who were too weak to fight for themselves."

"He sounds magnificent!"

"I thought so," the Princess replied. "So it did not matter to me that none of my family would speak to me and that my so-called friends cut me if they saw me as there was really nobody in my life except for Imbe."

As if she thought that Forella did not understand, she said,

"I soon realised that the people who were working with him and who followed his lead looked at me with suspicion."

"Why should they do that?"

"I was one of the 'upper classes' who they hated and with a good deal of justification." the Princess replied simply.

She made an expressive little gesture with her hands as she added,

"Their attitude did not matter to me any more than my family's for to me there was only Imbe! Imbe would come home to me and tell me how much he loved me and I could in his arms forget everything else however troublesome."

There was a smile on the Princess s lips as she went on,

"When you get to my age, child, you will soon realise that the only things that are worth remembering are the times of happiness and it means the times one gave and received love."

Forella went on to ask her more about the man she had married and to learn how he had fought valiantly and at times successfully against those who tried to suppress him.

"But they caught him in the end," the Princess said sadly. "Some small mistake made by one of the men he trusted gave them a chance to sentence him to death."

"Oh, no!"

Forella gave a cry of horror.

"Yes, they killed my Imbe and would not even allow me to say 'goodbye' to him before he died."

"That was cruel and heartless."

"They were afraid that, if they allowed him any concessions, he would somehow manage to escape at the last moment. He had always led a charmed life and they had begun to think that he was indestructible."

"It must have been – terrible for you."

"It was thought that I too should be taken to prison," the Princess carried on quietly, "and I knew that if that happened, even if I was not publicly condemned to death, I should die."

"And the Prince saved you?" Forella asked as if she already knew the answer.

"Yes, János appeared just when I was desperate and took me away from Hungary before anybody could realise what was happening and brought me to England."

She sighed before she continued,

"There was always a very real chance that the Hungarian Government would ask for my repatriation so he brought me here to live very quietly, hoping that, as nobody had heard of me and they could not find me, they would soon forget my very existence and I think that is what has happened."

"It is the most thrilling and exciting story I have ever heard," Forella exclaimed, "and I greatly admire you for your bravery."

"I do not want to be admired for anything except for giving the most controversial man in my country great happiness all the years we were together," the Princess said simply.

She was silent for a moment before she added,

"Now I want only to die so that I can be with him again."

"Which you will be," Forella cried. "Papa was always quite certain that when he died he would be with my mother."

"If one loves someone enough, there is no possibility that one could ever lose them," the Princess said quietly.

Then, as if she felt that she had talked enough about herself, she said,

"And that is what I would wish for my dear wonderful János, that he should find love."

"I thought he was married," Forella queried.

"He is," the Princess answered. "It was an arranged marriage when he was very young and it has not brought him any happiness."

She spoke in a suppressed way, as if she did not wish to say anything more and, because Forella was aware of what she was feeling, she said tactfully,

"It seems wrong that anybody so handsome and so kind should not be happy. I am sure somewhere there must be a woman waiting for him, as your husband was waiting for you and who will – bring him everything he deserves."

"That is what I pray for every morning and every night," the Princess said. "In point of fact every time I think of him."

*

When she retired to bed that night, Forella found herself thinking about the Prince and being surprised at learning that he was so different from what she had supposed.

Because he was surrounded by socialites like her uncle and aunt, the Earl and Lady Esme and all the other guests she had met at The Castle, she had thought that, although he had been kind to her, he too enjoyed the sort of life that her father had laughed at.

"Who wants to go to Buckingham Palace?" he had said once to her mother.

"I would like to go there just once," her mother replied, "and see if it is as grand and as glamorous as I have always understood it to be."

"You will see a lot of dressed-up fools," her father replied, "waiting for a Royal smile or a pat on the hand like a lot of sea lions waiting for fish."

Her mother had laughed.

"That is very scathing, darling."

"It is the truth," he said. "Men and women who you would think had some brain in their heads would crawl from here to the North Pole for the chance of receiving a Royal favour or, better still, a bit of metal they call a medal to hang on their chests."

"You are not to talk like that in front of Forella," her mother had protested.

"Why not?" her father asked, "When the time comes, which you are determined it shall, for her to be presented to Her Majesty the Queen she can make up her own mind if it is the most exciting thing that ever happened to her or whether she would rather be racing me on a horse who needs exercise along a beach stretching out for miles in front of us."

Her mother laughed and jumped up to say,

"We will both race you!"

After that any more talk about Buckingham Palace had been forgotten.

But her father's mockery of it had remained in Forella's mind and she had come to England feeling prejudiced against the Society life she was to lead with her uncle and aunt.

What had happened when the Earl of Sherburn had come to her bedroom by mistake had only confirmed her belief that her father had been right and everything to do with Society was unpleasant and even rather frightening.

Now what she had learnt about the Prince made her revise her opinion of him.

'It is because he is Hungarian,' she told herself. 'I know when I am talking to him that he is perceptive like my Mama. He understands what I am feeling and what I am thinking as no ordinary Englishman would ever be able to do.'

*

The following day, something else happened that made her see once again how different the Prince was.

She had been in the garden and had picked some lovely and heavily scented yellow roses for the Princess.

Carrying them in her hand, she was about to go into the drawing room when she heard somebody talking inside.

She wondered who it could be and if it would be a mistake for her to intrude.

Then she heard a man saying in French,

"Don't worry, *Princesse*, I am glad you called me, but it is nothing serious."

Forella then knew that it was the Doctor who was with the Princess and she thought that, if he was prescribing for her, she should wait outside until he had left.

At the same time she was surprised that he was speaking French, but she supposed it was easier to make himself understood as the Princess was not entirely proficient in English.

Then, as she would have turned away from the door, she heard him continue,

"The 'Poor Lady', there is nothing much I can do for her except to keep her quiet. I have given her something to make her sleep and, when she wakes, she will have forgotten what has happened."

At his words Forella was still.

'Poor Lady' were the words that Mrs. Newman used and, if the Doctor was prescribing for one of the servants, he would not have used that expression.

Because she was curious, she then walked into the drawing room and the Princess looked up to say in rather halting English,

"Oh, here you are, my child, I want you to meet with Dr. Bouvais, who attends me and is always a welcome visitor professionally or otherwise."

"Your Highness is very kind," the Doctor smiled.

He held out his hand to Forella, saying,

"*Enchanté, mademoiselle.*"

Not only the way he spoke but the way he looked made Forella realise that he was in fact French and she answered him in his own language, saying,

"I am delighted to meet you, *monsieur.*"

"I was told that you are Hungarian," he said in surprise, "but you speak French like a Parisian."

"That is a compliment he has never paid me," the Princess said. "My guest, *monsieur*, is a very talented young lady."

"And a very excellent rider," the Doctor said. "The whole village is talking of how they have never seen one of the Prince's horses ridden by a lady before."

Forella, who had no idea that anyone had noticed her outside The Manor, hoped it would not be dangerous.

Then she told herself she was certain that the Prince's idea that she should write to her uncle and say she was safe would prevent him from having any enquiries made about her.

"I must now leave you, *madame*," the Doctor said.

He kissed the Princess's hand in the French fashion, paid Forella a compliment with an unmistakable look of admiration in his eyes and left.

Forella gave the Princess the roses, saying as she did so,

"Surely it is very unusual to have a French Doctor living in the village?"

The Princess laughed.

"Surely you realise that he is another of dear János's lame ducks?"

"There is some reason for his being in Little Ledbury?"

"Of course," the Princess said. "Practically everyone round here has a reason for burying themselves in this dead-and-alive hole. As you can guess, I am extremely curious as to why you are here."

Forella looked away from her and chimed in quickly,

"Please tell me about the Doctor."

"Why not?" the Princess asked. "He makes no secret to me at any rate that if it was not for János he would have stood trial in France and doubtless would have received a sentence of several years' imprisonment."

"What did he do?" Forella asked.

The Princess shrugged her shoulders.

"He did not tell me the details, but my guess is that he performed an illegal operation or else the patient died and it was discovered."

Forella did not speak and the Princess went on,

"But whatever happened, I am totally sure he was not really to blame for a kinder more considerate man I have never met. He is also very intelligent and, while it is very pleasant for me to have him here, I cannot help feeling that he is wasted."

Forella had a great deal to think about when she was alone and she thought once again that it was rather like a play taking place in front of her eyes, but very different from the one she had watched at The Castle.

Then she could see all too clearly the Prince spiriting the Princess away from Hungary and making sure that she was not only comfortable but safe in his beautiful Manor House.

It was not surprising that the Doctor too was grateful for what he had done for him.

She asked herself how many other people the Prince had helped and was certain that one of them was Thomas.

'I hope he will tell me his story,' she thought, 'or perhaps the Princess will.'

But there was another question that she longed to know the answer to.

'Who is the 'Poor Lady?'

And, if she was living in the house, why had she not seen her?

*

It was on Wednesday that what Forella was expecting arrived.

It came by post chaise from London and, as soon as she saw what had been brought up to her bedroom, she thought it was typical of the Prince's forethought and his eye for detail.

There were two trunks on each of which was stamped a coronet over the letter 'R'.

Mrs. Newman and one of the housemaids had come to unpack them and, when they were unstrapped, Forella saw the clothes that the Prince had so kindly bought for her.

"I was just beginning to think, my Lady, that your luggage would never turn up," Mrs. Newman exclaimed when the trunks were opened. "It's these transportation difficulties that cause the trouble despite the fact that there are trains running from the coast to London now, which should make things easier."

Forella did not speak and she went on,

"Nasty dirty things they are too. I wouldn't risk my life in one of them."

Forella did not bother to reply, because she was looking at the gowns and thinking that they were more attractive and would suit her better than those her aunt had bought.

The Marchioness had been intent on making Forella look sensational so as to catch the eye of some prospective husband.

The Prince, on the other hand, she felt must have used his Hungarian instinct to know what would suit her best and what in his own words would then be a 'suitable frame for her beauty'.

The gowns were comparatively simple, but they had a distinction that she felt made them different from those she had seen on anyone else.

They were not the simple white of an English *debutante*, but were instead the colours of the alpine flowers that filled the Steppes after the snows had gone and which her mother had described to her so often.

The soft blues, pinks and golden yellows seemed to have a natural life of their own and remained unspoilt by the touch of humans.

Every gown was original in design and so attractive that Forella longed to see herself at once dressed in each one of them.

She decided first to try on a gown of soft green that seemed to accentuate the green of her eyes and make her skin dazzlingly white.

As Mrs. Newman buttoned her into it, she commented,

"Now you look, my Lady, like a breath of spring and it's somethin' you've brought to us ever since you've been here at The Manor."

"Thank you, Mrs. Newman," Forella replied in surprise.

"It be true, my Lady. When I hears you laugh and sees you runnin' down the stairs, you makes me feel as if I was young again myself and that's the truth!"

"You could not say anything kinder or nicer," Forella responded with a smile.

Because she wanted to show the Princess her new gown, she hurried along the landing.

Then, as she reached the top of the stairs, she realised that there was someone outside the front door.

She paused and then, as she saw a man walking into the hall, she felt her heart leap.

It was the Prince who she had been so hoping would come to see her.

She was about to call out, but there was no need.

As if what she was feeling drew him to her, he looked up and smiled when he saw her looking over the banisters.

She started off quickly down the stairs and he was watching her progress, waiting until she reached the hall.

Then he put out both his hands to take hers.

"You are all right?" he asked at once.

"Yes, and so very very glad to see you!" Forella answered. "The Princess and I thought perhaps you had forgotten us."

"It would be just impossible for me to forget you," he replied, "and may I say that you are looking very lovely."

Forella glanced down at her gown.

"It has just arrived — and I am so glad that — I can show it to you."

"It really suits you."

"That is what I thought and I felt, although I suppose it is an impossibility, that you had chosen it — especially for me."

"Shall I say I described what I wanted and what you looked like to someone who I knew would understand?"

"You are so – clever," Forella said, "as well as being so – very kind."

The way she said the last words made the Prince say,

"I have a feeling that my cousin has been talking to you."

"It was very interesting to hear what she told me."

"I might have guessed no woman can keep a secret," the Prince remarked provocatively as they walked towards the drawing room.

"I have kept mine," Forella told him in a low voice, "and please, you must tell me what is happening."

"Of course," he answered, "but first I must greet my cousin."

They went into the drawing room and the Princess gave a cry of joy at seeing the Prince.

"János!" she exclaimed. "I was so afraid you would go back to London without coming to see us."

"I had to wait until my last guest had departed," he replied, "and, I must say, somewhat reluctantly."

"That is what I suspected must have happened," the Princess said. "They impose on you, as we all do."

"That is not true. And even if it is, I like it!"

"Then that is all that matters," the Princess replied.

Then, as she looked at Forella for the first time, she exclaimed,

"Your clothes have arrived. Oh, I am glad. And what a pretty gown. You look beautiful in it, does she not, János?"

"I have just been telling her so," the Prince answered.

As he spoke, his eyes met Forella's, and for some reason that she could not understand, she found it hard to look away.

He had ridden over, as she might well have expected, and she thought that in his highly polished boots and cutaway coat he looked so smart and exceedingly handsome that he might have stepped out of a painting of a Georgian Buck.

She knew that, however conventionally dressed he might be, he did not look English.

There was something dashingly foreign about him that she could not put into words.

Newman came hurrying into the drawing room and behind him was one of the footmen carrying a tray on which there was a bottle of champagne in a silver ice cooler.

"Are we toasting anything special today?" the Princess asked.

"We are celebrating that you look so much better than I have seen you for some time, Cousin Maria," the Prince replied, "and that Forella looks happy."

"I *am* happy!" Forella exclaimed.

"And so am I," the Princess interposed. "These last few days I have been more amused by Forella than I have been for years."

"That is what I wanted you to say."

Newman poured out the champagne and, when they each had a glass of it in their hands, the Prince raised his,

"To happiness," he said simply. "What could be a more important toast for us all?"

He drank the champagne in his glass as he spoke, then put it down on a table and said,

"Will you allow me, Cousin Maria, to take Forella out into the garden? I have one or two personal things to discuss with her."

"Yes, of course," the Princess replied, "but be careful she does not spoil her new gown."

"Of course I will be very careful of it," the Prince answered mock-seriously.

They went out through the French window into the garden and, as they walked across the green lawn, Forella insisted,

"What has happened? You must tell me."

"I can give you the best answer to that question," he replied, "by saying 'nothing'!"

"Nothing?"

"I think your uncle was surprised and your aunt very angry when they read your note."

"And the Earl?"

"I imagine your aunt showed it to him for he certainly seemed more cheerful at the end of the day than he was at the beginning and he spent every moment with Lady Esme until her husband arrived."

As the Prince finished, he saw that Forella was staring at him in sheer astonishment.

"Her – husband?" she asked, as if she thought that she could not have heard him aright. "Do you mean to – say that Lady Esme is – married?"

"Of course she is married, I thought that you knew," the Prince said. "Her husband is Sir Richard Meldrum, a very distinguished Diplomat."

"But I had no idea," Forella exclaimed. "Then, if she is married – why was she – flirting with the Earl? And why did he go to her – bedroom?"

The innocence of the questions made the Prince draw in his breath.

Then he said,

"I think it is a mistake, Forella, for you to be interested in or to worry about those who you have left behind for your new life. You and I know the power of thought and perhaps by thinking of them too much you will attract their attention to yourself."

Forella gave a little cry of horror.

"That is something I do not want – and I am sure you are right."

She thought before she continued,

"When we were in India, Papa told me that some Indians would know either by thought or instinct when something had occurred some hundreds of miles away at the very time it was happening."

"That is true," the Prince said, "so I want you to promise me to stop thinking first about your uncle and aunt and secondly about the Earl. There is no reason for him ever to encroach on your life again,"

"Are you saying," Forella asked after a moment, "that I should stay here – forever?"

"No, of course not," the Prince replied. "I have plans for you, although I would rather not talk about them at the moment."

He knew that she looked at him curiously and he then said,

"I have asked you to trust me."

"I do trust you," Forella replied. "How can I possibly do anything else when you have been so kind to me? In the future I will not only – guard my tongue but also my – thoughts."

The Prince laughed,

"I am sure that is very sensible and the great art of disguise is to think yourself into the part that you have to play."

"That is what I am trying to do," Forella said. "The Princess is, I know, convinced that I am Hungarian and so is everybody else in the house."

"You are Hungarian!"

"At the same time I have never been in Hungary and I am always afraid of making a – mistake."

"What has happened to that bright intelligence that you told me was so very precious?" the Prince asked.

"Now you are trying to frighten me," Forella replied. "However, as I have been lucky so far – I am sure I shall be – lucky in the future."

"I am sure you will," he said smiling.

"My luck is all due to you," Forella answered in a low voice, "and I shall never never forget that you brilliantly saved me when I was – alone and frightened – from having to go back ignominiously – to The Castle and – marry the Earl."

"Forget it, forget it all!" the Prince urged her.

He spoke violently and Forella said meekly,

"I will try – because you have asked me to – and I want to please you."

"You *do* please me," the Prince said, "and I only wish I could stay and see you wearing the other gowns I have chosen for you."

"You – you are – leaving us?"

It was almost a cry.

"I have to go to London today," the Prince said, "but I will come back as soon as I can."

"Promise me you will."

Forella did not know why, but she wanted to hold onto him to prevent him from going and she so wanted him to stay.

"I promise," the Prince said, "and perhaps next time I shall be able to stay for longer."

"You know how much it will mean to the – Princess."

Then, as if she could not help herself, she added,

"And to – me!"

The Prince did not respond and she felt that there was a strange expression on his face.

As they turned to walk back to the house, several doves rose from the bushes just ahead of them and flew away with a flutter of their wings.

"I now remember just what it is I wanted to ask you," Forella said, "Both the Doctor and Mrs. Newman mentioned somebody they both referred to as the 'Poor Lady'. Who do they mean?"

Even as she spoke she felt that she had made a mistake. The Prince was frowning and there was a grim expression on his face that she had not seen before.

Then, when she wanted to say that she was sorry she had been so curious and should not have been so inquisitive, he replied in a voice that had no expression in it whatsoever,

"They were speaking of my wife!"

CHAPTER SIX

For a moment it was impossible for Forella to speak.

Then in a voice that did not sound like her own she managed to repeat,

"Your – *wife*?"

She had never imagined for one moment, it had simply never crossed her mind that the Princess might be living in The Manor or even be in England.

And yet now it seemed to be a reasonable place for the Prince to bring his wife, who was obviously an invalid.

They had now reached the house, but, instead of going in through the French window by which they had left it, the Prince suddenly turned round.

Taking Forella by the arm, he walked back into the garden, across the green lawn and through some shrubs into a part that she had visited only once.

It was wilder than the rest of the garden with shrubs rather than flowers and at the end of it was a small summerhouse that Forella imagined was seldom used.

The Prince paused and she saw that just under the thatched roof, which was covered with climbing roses, there was a wooden seat with cushions on it.

It was all part of the perfection that was so evident in everything to do with him that a servant must every day in the summer put the cushions on the wooden seat in case anybody should wish to go there.

But now it was impossible to think of anything but what the Prince had just told her and how surprising it was to be under the same roof as his wife.

They sat down on the seat.

Then he began,

"I want to tell you about my wife, Forella, and I would rather do so myself than that you should hear a garbled version from someone else."

Because she felt that there was a note of pain in his voice, Forella said quickly,

"Please do not tell me – if you would – rather not. I am sorry if I seemed – curious."

"It is understandable."

He did not smile, but sat staring out in front of him with what Forella felt were unseeing eyes.

Then, after what seemed to her to be an uncomfortable pause, he started his story,

"I married when I was very young to the daughter of a neighbouring landowner whose family was of equal standing to mine. Although the marriage was arranged by my father and the father of the bride, when I saw Gisella, she was so exquisitely beautiful that I fell very much in love with her."

For some reason which she did not understand, Forella felt an odd emotion inside her when he spoke of his wife.

Although she did not say anything to him or move, she knew perceptively that he was aware that she was listening intently.

"It was only after we were married, because we had seen so little of each other before," the Prince said, "that I realised Gisella was very young for her age and in fact in many ways she was completely childlike."

He gave a sigh that seemed to come from the very depths of his being before he went on,

"That is indeed the whole story. Gisella never grew up and, although I think her parents must have been aware of her affliction, they were so delighted at the marriage that they said nothing that might have prevented it."

Forella made a little exclamation, but she did not speak and the Prince continued,

"It was only when I understood that Gisella was unable to concentrate on anything for more than a few seconds and that a flower or a butterfly would amuse her while I as a man really had no place in her life, that I faced the truth."

"Was there no – chance that she could – get better?" Forella managed to ask.

"As you can imagine," he replied, "I took her to every Doctor in Hungary, Austria and France, but they only confirmed what I knew already, that she was a child who would never grow up."

He paused before he continued,

"She had, they told me, suffered brain damage, perhaps at birth, perhaps through being dropped as a baby, they could not be sure of the reason."

Now there was a note of pain in the Prince's voice that was unmistakable and, as Forella instinctively put out her hand towards him, he said in a sharper tone,

"That is not all."

"What else?"

"As Gisella grew older, her temper became uncontrollable and occasionally dangerous."

"Oh – no!"

The exclamation of horror seemed to burst from Forella's lips.

"That is why," the Prince went on as if she had not spoken, "she always has to have two Nurses with her and cannot be allowed to see anybody else. She may go for a week, perhaps a month or two, without an attack and then when it comes it is frightening."

Again he took a deep breath before he resumed,

"That is all, but I wanted you to know the truth from me."

"I am glad – you told me," Forella said, "but it – hurts me to think what you must have – suffered."

"I do not want sympathy," he said in a hard voice. "I have so many compensations in life and I am very grateful for all of them."

She thought he was referring to his horses, his wealth and his position both in Hungary and in England, but now for the first time she realised that beneath all the artificial trappings, the glitter and the glamour, he must be a lonely man.

"In the same way that you have – helped so – many people," Forella said softly, "I – wish I could – help you."

For the first time since they had sat down in the summerhouse he turned to look at her and now there was an expression in his eyes that she did not understand as he said,

"I am making arrangements to send you away to Hungary where you will be safe. For if your relatives will not welcome you, then mine will."

"To Hungary?" Forella exclaimed almost beneath her breath. "But – it is so far – and I should be frightened – please can I not stay here? I am so happy with the Princess – and I can also – sometimes see you."

Her eyes were raised upwards and, as the Prince looked down at her, she felt as if quite suddenly his grey eyes seemed to grow until everything vanished and they filled the world, the sky and the whole Universe!

For a second – or a century – time stood still.

Then he said in a tone that she had not heard before,

"For God's sake, do not make things more difficult than they are already. You have to go. You must be aware why."

Forella gave a little gasp.

Then, with a movement almost as violent as the tone of his voice, the Prince rose from the seat and walked away quickly.

He had vanished between the shrubs almost before she could realise exactly what was happening.

Only when he was out of sight, and yet his voice seemed still to be ringing on the air, did she realise what he had said and she knew that she loved him.

*

The Prince drove his horses through Regent's Park and then North towards St. John's Wood where there were some small attractive houses standing in their own gardens.

He drew up at one of the larger of them and handed the reins to his groom.

"Walk the horses, Higson," he ordered. "I shall not be long."

"Very good, Your 'Ighness."

The Prince stepped down and raised the silver knocker on the door.

After a short wait it was opened by a maid wearing a lace apron and starched white cap.

She looked surprised at seeing him and bobbed a curtsey.

"Good morning, Your 'Ighness, *m'mselle's* not expectin' you."

"I know that," the Prince replied entering the small hall.

He put down his top hat and gloves and the maid waiting at the foot of the stairs asked,

"Will Your 'Ighness go up to *m'mselle* or shall I tell her you're here?"

The Prince paused for a moment before he replied,

"Tell *mademoiselle* that I wish to speak to her in the sitting room."

"Very good, Your 'Ighness."

The Prince walked into the sitting room that was beautifully furnished and had windows overlooking both the front and the back of the house.

Besides the flowers in vases, and there was a profusion of them, there were also huge baskets of orchids.

One of them, of purple cattleya, completely filled the fireplace, while another on a table by the window partially obscured the view of the garden.

The Prince put down on a small side table two parcels that he had carried into the house.

Then he stood still in a way that was not quite natural and there was an expression on his face that Forella would have known perceptively was one of pain.

It was nearly five minutes before there was the sound of feet running swiftly down the stairs, the door opened, and Lucille du Pré came into the room.

The grace of her body and the way she moved would have told any observer who was not aware of her fame that she was a ballerina.

She was also beautiful with almost perfect features and huge eyes that were accentuated by mascara on her long eyelashes.

She was wearing only a *négligee* over her nightgown and her dark hair, which reached to below her waist, was tied back with pink satin ribbon.

"*Mon cher*, what a surprise!" she exclaimed in French and then held out her arms to the Prince.

He prevented her from coming any nearer by taking both of her hands in his and kissing them one after the other.

"I did not expect you so early," Lucille said, "and actually I am angry with you because you have not been to see me for what seems a very long time."

"I have, however, heard of your triumph," the Prince replied.

"It is *fantastique*, is it not? The newspapers have written about me and the Director has gone on his knees to beg me to extend my contract."

She spoke with an elation and a lilt in her voice that told him how much it meant to her.

"I am glad, so very glad," the Prince said, "and I have brought you a present."

"I should thank you for the flowers and for the present you sent me on the first night."

"This is a different present."

He turned to the side table, picked up the square velvet-covered box and opened it.

Lucille gave a gasp.

Inside in the centre of the box was a diamond necklace, which glittered against a black velvet background and there were two drop earrings and a wide bracelet to match.

"*C'est magnifique*," Lucille cried. "How can I tell you just how thrilled I am to possess anything so fabulous?"

Again she held out her arms, but the Prince avoided them and picked up the other parcel he had placed on the side table.

This consisted of some sheets of parchment tied with red tape, which the Prince handed to Lucille, saying,

"My other present for you is the deeds to this house."

She stared at him, but did not speak and he went on,

"I have also deposited a sum of money in your Bank, which will keep you in comfort for a very long time, even if you are not earning the astronomical fees that you are getting now."

Lucille was still.

Then she looked up at him to ask,

"Why are you giving me all these things?"

"They are to thank you for the happiness we have found together."

"For three years," she murmured.

"As you say, for three years."

There was silence.

Then Lucille asked him,

"Are you saying that you are leaving me?"

"We both agreed," the Prince said quietly, "that if at any time either of us wished to break what has been a very close and very perfect friendship and then we would part without explanations or recriminations."

"I know we said that," Lucille replied, "but I did not think, I never imagined – "

She stopped for a moment and then she said,

"What you are telling me is that there is – somebody else."

"There is, but I have no wish to speak of it," the Prince replied. "I only want to wish you great happiness, Lucille, which I know you will find and, of course, your continued success and the acclaim which has already reverberated throughout London."

Lucille did not answer. She only stared down at the jewels in the box that she held in her hands.

The Prince put the deeds back on the side table from where he had taken them.

Then he looked at her for a long moment before he said very quietly,

"Goodbye, Lucille, and thank you."

Only as she heard the door close behind him did she seem to come out of the trance that had held her silent.

"Wait! Wait!" she called out.

She ran across the room to pull open the door that he had closed.

But he had already gone from the house.

As she reached the front door, he was already driving away and she had only a glimpse of his back disappearing down the road.

It was then that she flung the jewel box and its contents down on the floor and burst into tears.

*

"I wonder when János will come and see us again," the Princess said as Forella closed the book that she had been reading aloud.

She realised as the Princess spoke that she had not really been listening and, if she was honest, she knew that her mind too had been on other things or rather on one thing.

Ever since the Prince had gone, she had found it impossible to think of anything but him.

When she had finally returned to The Manor, she had found that he had already left and the Princess was grumbling that his visit had been so short.

"Now we may not see him for weeks," she said, "but I suppose I must not complain. It is only through his kindness that I am safe here."

"I suppose he is – going to – London," Forella said, finding it hard to speak.

"Of course," the Princess replied, "and that means his social friends, including the Prince and Princess of Wales, will be waiting there for him eagerly, just as we are."

When she had gone to bed that night, Forella had lain awake thinking of the Prince and knowing that her love for him had increased until she felt that with every beat of her heart she loved him more.

She told herself it was ridiculous, absurd and something that she should not have allowed to happen.

But she knew that just as she was so perceptive about other things, her instinct had drawn her to the Prince from the very first moment she had seen him.

While her mind had tried to decry him as being part of the Social world that she disliked and mistrusted, her heart had told her even then that he was very different.

She had fought against the magnetism of him and the fact that he was the most handsome man she had ever seen.

But even before the people who had trusted him had told her of his exceptional kindness, sympathy and understanding, she had known that after he had brought her to The Manor, she had been waiting, like the Princess, eagerly and excitedly to see him again.

Today, when she had gone into the hall, her heart had turned several somersaults at the sight of him.

She knew that, if she had been truthful, she would have admitted then that what she was feeling for him was love and, although he had not said it in so many words, she knew as if it was written in letters of fire that he loved her.

'How is it possible?' her brain argued. 'I must have been – mistaken.'

But, when his grey eyes had looked into hers, and he told her that he was sending her away, she knew that the reason was quite simple, it was love.

However Forella did not deceive herself for one moment that there could ever be a happy ending to their story.

In the first place, the Prince was married and secondly, even if he was free, what could she possibly offer Prince János Kovác, with his wealth, his power, his possessions and most of all himself?

'I am just a nobody, ignorant of his world and anything he is interested in except horses,' she thought, 'When he sends me to Hungary he will – forget about me – while I will – never ever forget him.'

Moreover she had to suppose that the Prince's affection for her must be only a transitory one, when the Princess had told her of his successes in London, Paris and everywhere else in the world.

"He is admired and respected," the Princess had told her, "not only by the Statesmen and sportsmen of each country but also by their beautiful women."

Because the Princess had little to think about at the moment except for her cousin who had saved her from imprisonment and maybe death, she pored over the Social columns of the newspapers to find out what Prince János was doing, who he was entertaining and who was entertaining him.

She cut every mention of his name out of the newspapers.

There was one drawer, Forella discovered, in the drawing room that was already half-filled with press cuttings, articles from magazines and artists' sketches of The Castle and of the Prince himself.

He would more often than not be sketched leading in the winner of some famous horse race which he had won the Cup for and the prize money against competitors from the most famous stables in the country.

Because it was a bittersweet pleasure to talk about him, Forella encouraged the Princess to show her the newspaper reports and assisted her in finding others.

"Listen to this one," the Princess had said triumphantly today after the newspapers had arrived and she had immediately opened one, the *Court Circular*.

She read aloud,

"At the Duchess of Manchester's ball last night,

the Princess of Wales, looking radiantly beautiful in grey silk trimmed with Venetian lace, was talking to handsome Prince János Kovác.

Later the Prince, one of the most successful racehorse owners in Europe as well as in England, took in to supper the lovely Marchioness of Sheen, whose exquisite face has been immortalised in no less than three portraits to be exhibited in the Royal Academy this year."

The Princess put down the newspaper for a moment.

"The Marchioness of Sheen," she remarked reflectively. "She is a new beauty and I am prepared to wager quite a large sum of money that she will soon be a guest at The Castle."

"Does His Highness invite – only beautiful – women to stay with him?" Forella asked in a low voice.

"But of course," the Princess replied. "Why should he entertain plain ones? János, more than any other man, expects perfection."

She gave a little laugh.

"In his horses, in his houses and, of course, in his women!"

"His women!"

The words seemed to echo in Forella's mind and then repeat and repeat themselves all through the night.

The days, which before had been a delight now seemed to pass slowly while the nights seemed interminable.

Everywhere she looked, everything she heard and everything she thought seemed to be part of the Prince.

'He has taken possession of me,' she told herself.

While in a way it was a frightening thought, something alive and thrilling seemed to leap like a little flame within her almost as if he was touching her.

The days passed without his coming again to The Manor and so her elation began to die away.

The newspaper reports of the balls he attended and the Receptions at which he had been present told her how unimportant and insignificant she was in comparison and that the Prince had obviously forgotten her.

Perhaps he would remember her again when he received an answer from Hungary and then she would just find herself being sent there.

She would at least be safe from being taken back by her uncle and aunt and then forced to marry the Earl of Sherburn. But she would also be exiled from the Prince, the only person now who meant anything in her life.

'How can I – leave him, how can I – lose him?' she asked despairingly.

Yet she knew that, when he ordered her to go, she would leave and that would be the end of it.

As he had not told her that she must not mention his wife to the Princess, after three days of keeping the secret to herself, Forella said tentatively,

"When His Highness was – here, I asked him who was referred to as the – 'Poor Lady' and he told me it was – his wife."

The Princess gave a little sigh of relief.

"I am glad he told you," she replied. "I did not like to tell you myself for fear it would annoy him, but, because she is hidden here, I knew I should be safe from being sent back to Hungary and from those who wish to hurt me because they hated my husband."

She gave a little laugh before she added,

"Trust János to find the perfect hiding place for all sorts and conditions of people, like the Doctor, Thomas, myself and, of course, poor Gisella."

"Did you know her?" Forella asked.

"I have never actually spoken to her," the Princess replied, "because I had left home a long time before János married her, but I had seen her in the distance and thought her very beautiful and a very suitable bride for János until I learnt the truth."

She did not wait for Forella to reply but carried on,

"Oh, my poor dear János! How can this have happened to him of all people? I pray every night of my life that one day he will be free and have the family he has always wanted."

Her voice was very moving as she said,

"He needs sons to inherit his title and his vast possessions and daughters whom I know he would love and who would inevitably be very beautiful because he surrounds himself with nothing but beauty."

"It seems — cruel that — nothing can be — done," Forella faltered.

"Nothing at all," the Princess agreed. "They are tied 'until death do them part' and Dr. Bouvais informs me that the Princess may live for very much longer than János himself."

Forella wanted to cry out at the injustice of it, but she was afraid of betraying herself to the Princess, who she knew had no idea of her feelings for the Prince.

"Do you ever — visit the 'Poor Lady?'" she asked tentatively.

"No," the Princess replied. "János has asked me not to do so, as visitors could excite her, which would be a mistake."

"She has her doves?"

"Yes, her doves, although there are now far too many," the Princess replied sharply. "It is not safe for her to have any other animals, but doves can easily fly away."

There was no need for the Princess to say any more, for the Prince had already told her that his wife was violent at times.

But Forella felt that she was vividly conscious of the presence of the 'Poor Lady' in the other part of the house and she understood why there were so many servants.

Now she knew why they never spoke, except inadvertently, of the 'Poor Lady', who was shut away with her Nurses.

'It is a cruel Fate for her and even more cruel for him,' Forella thought.

Although she prayed for them both, as the days passed by and the Prince did not come to The Manor, her prayers became more and more despairing.

Then one morning when she was helping her dress, Mrs. Newman warned her,

"Now don't go wanderin' too far from the house, my Lady. I saw you yesterday from the windows walking up towards the wood."

"There is a lovely view from there," Forella replied.

"Well, it would be best if you kept to the garden."

"Why?"

There was silence.

Then Forella, feeling that something was wrong, asked quickly,

"'Why should you ask me to do that? What has happened?"

"Maybe I shouldn't mention it, my Lady," Mrs. Newman replied, "but then there's been a man snoopin' around the place, Thomas sees him hangin' about the stables and asks him what he's doin'. He said he was just a visitor who has lost his way."

Forella was listening intently, feeling frightened that the man might in some way concern her.

"Then one of the footmen," Mrs. Newman carried on, "says that, when he was a-goin' down to the village, the man was outside the gate and asks him questions about the house and who lives in it. Of course he told the man nothing. At the same time we all wants to know why he was so curious."

Forella felt her heart give a beat.

Despite the Prince's optimism, she had always felt that sooner or later when she did not return, her uncle would begin to grow impatient and feel that, as he was responsible, he must find her.

She had been so intent on thinking about the Prince and so happy and relaxed in the quiet and peace of The Manor that she now felt despairingly that she had been over-confident.

She was not safe, of course, she was not in any way safe since her uncle, who was a very conscientious man, would feel it his duty to go and find her.

Then she would be taken back to London, Aunt Kathie would immediately announce her engagement to the Earl of Sherburn and she would never be able to run away again.

'What can I do? *What can I do*?' she thought frantically.

She would have liked to discuss it with the Princess, but she thought it might upset her.

Anyway, how could she help, tied as she was to her chair and powerless when it came to a question of the Law?

The Prince would be powerless too, because, as Forella was well aware, a Guardian had complete and absolute power over his Ward.

If her uncle and aunt were still intent on her marrying the Earl, she would be married to him however much she might protest or however much he might dislike the idea.

Now in the face of danger she realised that the Prince was right in making arrangements for her to go to Hungary.

Once she was out of the country, no detective would be able to find her, so the sooner she left the better.

But in the meantime there was always the chance that it might be too late.

Before she went out through the front door where Thomas would be waiting for her with György, she ran into the library and quickly wrote a letter to the Prince.

"*Your Highness,*

There is a man hanging round the house asking questions. He is making everybody nervous and I feel sure it is someone Uncle George has sent to look for me.

Please come as soon as you can and tell me what I can do. I am frightened, very frightened, and I feel that only you can save me.

Forella."

She placed the note in an envelope, addressed it to the Prince at his London house and went out into the hall where Newman was waiting for her to leave.

"Will you have this posted immediately to the Prince?" she asked him.

Then she paused.

"I think it would be – quicker if – somebody took it to London. It will only take about two-and-a-half hours and I think that the Prince should have it at once."

Newman's impassive face expressed no surprise at her request.

"Yes, of course, my Lady," he replied. "I will arrange for one of the grooms to leave immediately."

"Thank you," Forella said and hurried outside to where György was waiting.

As she rode away on him with Thomas on another magnificent stallion belonging to the Prince, she said,

"I have heard that a man has been asking questions here. Have you seen him? What is he like?"

"I have seen him," Thomas replied, "but he has not spoken to me, I gather, although I may be mistaken, that he is not interested in the stables and that I am extremely thankful for, but in the house."

Forella felt her heart miss a beat before she said,

"You have no idea who he might be looking for?"

"None, my Lady," Thomas replied, "and he may well, of course, be just a nosey-parker, or perhaps a burglar 'casing the joint', as they say."

"I feel that a burglar would not ask questions and risk people noticing him," Forella said tentatively.

"No, I'm sure you are right, my Lady."

He was frowning, however, and Forella said impulsively,

"I expect you are aware that practically everyone here is hiding from something and so it concerns us all."

"That's right," Thomas agreed, "and I have no wish to be recognised."

"I thought – perhaps you were – hiding as I am," Forella ventured.

"Yes, I am hiding," Thomas replied, "and it is thanks entirely to His Highness that I am a free man."

As they were talking, Gyõrgy began to shy at anything that he noticed and Forella had to keep a tight rein on him.

"We'll let the horses have their heads, my Lady," Thomas said, "and talk later. I think they're jealous because we are not attending to them."

Forella laughed and let Gyõrgy gallop until she thought that he had worked off some of his freshness.

Then, when they were able to speak again, Thomas told her that he had been a trainer at Newmarket for a distinguished member of the Jockey Club.

One of his jockeys, desperately eager to win the Two Thousand Guineas, had, although Thomas was completely unaware of it, doped the horse that he was riding.

He had won the race, but another jockey, jealous of his success, had complained to the Stewards, who had instituted an enquiry.

The jockey, to save his face, had sworn that he was innocent and that it was Thomas, the trainer of the horse, who had actually doped the animal to make him go faster.

"It was one of those complicated cases," Thomas said drily, "and so the verdict rested simply on whose word the Stewards believed."

"And they did not believe you," Forella exclaimed.

"His Highness told me that they favoured the other jockey because I had been somewhat revolutionary in my training methods and had in the past, through no fault of my own, made several enemies amongst the other trainers."

He sighed and added in a low voice,

"There was every chance of my being humiliated and struck off the Register."

"That would have been grossly unfair," Forella cried.

"What happens on a Racecourse often is," Thomas said philosophically. "His Highness convinced me that the best thing I could do was not to face the enquiry but to resign from the position I held."

His voice deepened as he went on,

"He helped me write a letter protesting my innocence, but making it clear that I thought it best from the point of view of racing as a great sport, that there should be no scandal."

He gave a dry laugh.

"It was a clever letter and I understand my action was very much approved by the Jockey Club in general."

"So you came here," Forella quizzed him.

"Yes, His Highness brought me here and gave me some magnificent horses to look after, which has made life very much pleasanter for me than it might have been otherwise."

"And what of the future?" Forella asked.

Thomas smiled and she realised that it was something he seldom did.

"His Highness has promised me that, when everything has quietened down and there is no question of my being recognised, he will set me up as a trainer in Paris, where he has a large stable that he intends to make larger still."

Forella gave an exclamation of delight.

"That will be splendid for you."

"I am looking forward to it, my Lady, but His Highness insists on waiting for at least five years until I am forgotten at Newmarket and there is no possible way that in France I should be connected with a trainer whose method of racing was queried by the Jockey Club."

"I understand."

She thought how right the Princess had been in describing everybody at The Manor as the Prince's 'lame ducks'.

As they all had something to hide, it was very obvious that anybody asking questions and snooping about the place would make them nervous and anxious.

At the same time she was convinced that, as they had not been spied on before, it must be she who was responsible.

It was the search for her which had brought this man, who was making it difficult for Forella, the Princess, the Doctor and, for all she knew, a number of others, to sleep quietly at night.

'The Prince will settle everything when he comes back,' she thought.

She found herself thinking all the time how long it would be before the groom reached the house in London, what the Prince would then do when he read her note and how soon he would arrive at The Manor.

It was ten days now since she had last seen him, but she thought that to her it seemed like ten centuries.

She had the feeling that he was avoiding her and she kept remembering that he had said she was making things worse than they were already.

'But what exactly had he meant by that?'

Perhaps she had read into it something quite different from what he had intended.

Forella suddenly felt very young, very insecure and very ignorant.

After the strange life she had lived with her father and mother, what did she know of men like Prince János? And what, for that matter, did she know of England?

She had met Sultans and Chieftains, Arab Sheiks and men who lived only to fight, to plunder and to kill.

And yet, until she came to England, she had never met men like her uncle or the Earl and certainly never one like the Prince.

It had been difficult at first to think that they were real and not just elegantly dressed characters from a story.

But now, when she thought of the Prince, he was very real. She knew that just to be with him was a joy and a rapture that was impossible to express in words as it was something which had never happened to her before.

Then she laughed at herself for being so foolish as to think that she could mean anything to him personally.

She was just another of his 'lame ducks' to whom he had extended his patronage and his compassion.

'He is sorry for me, he pities me. To him I am not an attractive woman like the beautiful ladies who fill his house in London and his Castle and who amuse him as I am quite unable to do.'

At night she thought over every conversation she had had with the Prince and decided that she had been stupid to argue and undoubtedly bore him with her tirades against Society.

To him they must have seemed extremely revolutionary and presumptuous ideas on the part of a young girl.

'I should have just kept quiet and let him do the talking,' she chided herself.

She longed in despair, as many other women had done before her, to put back the clock and be totally different from what she had been.

It was impossible to sleep until the stars were fading away and there was only an hour left before dawn.

Then at last she did slip away into unconsciousness and dreamt that the Prince was there and that everything had changed. They were walking together, hand in hand and she was no longer afraid.

She awoke with a start and, because she felt restless, she got out of bed and pulled back the curtains.

Her bedroom looked out onto the garden and in the dawn light there was a faint mist over the stream and everything had a soft translucent quality and the stillness that came just before the dawn.

Then, as Forella stood there looking out and thinking, still enraptured by her dream, she looked down.

In the shadows of the bushes bordering part of the lawn there was something that seemed darker and bulkier than the slender boughs, the leaves and the blossoms.

It was difficult to see clearly, until, as she stared and something made her go on staring, she was aware that it was a man!

A man and she was sure that he was looking up at the windows of the house.

Although she could not see his face, she thought it was her window that he was staring at.

It was unlikely that he could see her and, because she was frightened, she stepped further back into the room.

Only as she did so, did she realise that she was trembling.

She was now absolutely certain that whoever her uncle had employed to seek her out had discovered that she was at The Manor disguised under a false name.

CHAPTER SEVEN

Walking back from the garden and into the house with some roses that she had picked for the Princess, Forella was thinking excitedly that the Prince might come today.

She was sure that he would not ignore her appeal, but she was afraid that he might not be in London, but perhaps watching his horses win on some distant Racecourse.

But, because there was a chance of seeing him, she had put on one of the prettiest gowns that he had sent her.

She knew as she looked in the mirror that her eyes were bright with excitement and an expression that made her shy because it was so unmistakably one of love.

It seemed impossible that she should love him so completely and so unexpectedly when she knew so little about him.

But her father had fallen in love with her mother the moment he saw her and her mother had felt the same about him.

"I thought that he was the most handsome man who I had ever seen," her mother told her. "Then, when he looked at me I felt as if my heart leapt out towards him and, although even now it still seems impossible, I fell in love."

'I understand,' Forella told herself, 'and just as Mama loved Papa all her life, so will I never be able to

~171~

love anybody else in the same way as I love Prince János.'

Then she remembered that the 'Poor Lady' was upstairs and felt as if there was a shadow over the sun.

At the moment the one thing more important than anything else was the possibility that she had been traced.

Unless the Prince could save her again, she would then be taken back to London and, after being scolded severely by her aunt, she would be forced to marry the Earl whether she wished it or not.

'If the Prince does not come by tomorrow, then perhaps I had better run away,' Forella pondered.

But how, after all the security and happiness of being at The Manor, she could no longer contemplate, as she had before, setting off on her own on György without knowing where she was going and with very little money.

'The Prince will come, I know he will come to me,' she told herself consolingly.

Then, as she walked through the French window into the drawing room, he was there!

She had not expected him so early and for a moment she felt that she had just stepped out of her dreams.

But he was real, he was human and he was standing looking at her with an expression in his eyes that made it impossible for her to breathe.

She had her back to the sun coming in through the window, the red lights in her hair were dancing like little tongues of flame and she looked exceedingly lovely.

After a minute Forella managed to murmur,

"You – are *here*!"

Her voice broke the spell between them and the Prince walked forward.

"Yes, I am here," he said in his deep voice. "I came as soon as I could."

"It is – so early," Forella said, "that the Princess will – not be ready to – see you."

She was not thinking of what she was saying.

She was aware only of how handsome he was and his nearness made her feel that shafts of sunshine were piercing her body and becoming, as they touched her heart, little flames of fire.

"It is you I want to see," the Prince said quietly. "But first I want to find out exactly what has been happening here and what is the reason for it."

As he finished speaking, to Forella's surprise a young boy came running into the room.

"I have found them, Uncle János," he cried excitedly, "and now I want to use them."

The Prince smiled at him and said,

"Miklos, let me first present you to a very charming lady. Forella, this is my nephew and he has come to England to go to school, where he will in future be known as 'Michael'."

Forella held out her hand and Miklos, who was about twelve years old, bowed over it in the most elegant manner before he said as if he wanted her to join in his excitement,

"Do you know what I have here?"

He was carrying a box in his hand and Forella answered him,

"I have no idea."

"Uncle János tells me that it is a telescope that was used at the Battle of Trafalgar and, as I am going to be a sailor when I grow up, I want to know how to use one myself."

"Actually," the Prince said, "there are two telescopes in the box and I think you might show this lady how to use one."

"Of course," Miklos agreed.

The Prince looked at Forella.

"Take Miklos into the garden," he said, "and, when I have seen Thomas, who I have sent for, I will know more and we can talk about it."

Forella put the roses she was carrying down on a side table and, as she did so, Miklos ran ahead out of the French window and into the garden.

"Do not be frightened," the Prince said in a low voice, "you know I will look after you."

"I saw the man last night – looking up at – my window," Forella answered. "I am sure Uncle George – must have sent him to find me."

"Trust me," the Prince replied, "and perhaps it is not as dangerous as you fear.

"I hope – not."

She wanted to stay with him and she wanted to go on talking just so that she could be near him.

Then there came a knock on the door and she guessed that it must be Thomas.

Without saying any more, she went quickly through the window into the garden in search of Miklos.

When she joined him, she said,

"You must tell me all about the history of your telescopes."

"Uncle János says they are very precious and also at the time they were the strongest telescopes that had ever been made."

He opened the box and Forella looking down saw two telescopes lying side by side.

"I think," she said, "if we go towards the wood there is a good view from there and we can find out how far we can see with them."

"Yes, please let us do that," Miklos agreed at once.

He was a good-looking little boy and Forella thought as she had before how cruel it was that the Prince could not have had a son of his own.

She was quite certain that if he did have one, the boy would be very handsome.

The Prince would want to teach him to ride as well as he did and to take part in all the other pursuits he was proficient at.

She thought it must be a poor substitute for him to interest himself in his sister's children and she had learnt from the Princess that he had no brothers.

"Where are you going to school?" she asked Miklos.

"Uncle János has arranged for me to go to Eton," he answered. "He says it is the best school in the world and I am very fortunate. But first I am going to a crammer in London."

"I am sure you will enjoy Eton as much as my father did," Forella replied.

By this time they had reached the steps at the end of the garden that led up into the wood.

When they had climbed up a little way, Forella thought it would be wiser for them not to go any further, just in case they encountered the man who had been watching the house.

She therefore stopped and said,

"Let us discover how far we can see from here."

Miklos was only too willing.

He put the box down on the ground, took out the two telescopes and handed one to her.

"I expect you know how to adjust it," he said.

"I think so," Forella replied with a smile.

She took it from him and looked out over the valley to realise that there was a heat haze which made it difficult to see very clearly.

She swung the telescope round towards the house, wishing, as she did so, that she could see the Prince.

Then she had an idea.

"I tell you what we will do, Miklos," she said. "If we both look through the telescopes we can see the white doves on the roof. We will have a competition to see who can count the most."

"I like that!" Miklos exclaimed. "And what will be the prize?"

"You will have to ask your Uncle János that," Forella said. "Tell me when you are ready to start."

"I am ready now."

"Very well," Forella replied, putting the telescope to her right eye and shutting the other one. "One — two — three — *Go!*"

The telescopes were strong and she could see the white doves clearly fluttering round the gables.

Then she realised that there were a number of them on one of the windowsills on the third floor and she knew it must be where the 'Poor Lady' fed them.

Without thinking, she began to count the ones that were obviously pecking at something on the sill.

Then, as she did so, someone came to the window.

It was a woman. Forella could see her face quite clearly and knew that she was looking at the Prince's wife.

There was no doubt that she was still pretty, but it was a child's face and even at such a distance Forella thought that she looked very very young.

Then, as she stared at her, forgetting for the moment about the doves, there was suddenly a flutter of wings and she was aware that the Princess was now leaning a long way out of the window.

It passed through Forella's mind that it was dangerous and that she might fall.

Even as she thought it, she saw the 'Poor Lady's' hands reaching out into space, as if she was trying to save herself and realised with horror that she was not falling but being pushed!

There was a man behind her and she could see his arms and his shoulders.

Then, as the 'Poor Lady' fell from the window into space, Forella felt she could almost hear the scream that must have come from her lips.

It was all so quick, there was a flutter of white that was like the wings of the doves and then the 'Poor Lady' had vanished.

It seemed impossible that it had happened!

Then, as Forella still looked, there was a man in the window and she could see his face quite clearly.

It was somebody she had never seen before with dark hair and a heavy black moustache.

He looked down at the ground, then moved back and disappeared inside.

As Forella gasped at what she had seen, Miklos, beside her, exclaimed,

"Somebody fell out the window! Did you see? She fell! I saw her!"

"That – is what I – thought."

"And there was a man at the window. Why did he not save her?"

"Perhaps it was – impossible to do – so."

Then, because what she had seen was so frightening, and at the same time it seemed as if it could not really have happened and had just been a trick of the telescope, she said,

"I-I think, Miklos, we should – go back to the house."

"We must go and tell Uncle János what we have seen," Miklos replied. "Do you think the lady who fell has been hurt?"

"I don't – know," Forella answered, "but we must – find out."

Her words were almost incoherent.

Then it was impossible to say anything more because they had reached the lawn and she started to run.

Miklos ran beside her, grasping his telescope and the box, which he had remembered to pick up.

Only as they drew nearer to the house did Forella go a little slower so as to catch her breath.

She wanted to reach the Prince, but at the same time she was afraid that the whole thing had been some strange illusion.

Yet she knew that she had actually seen it happen and so had Miklos.

They reached the drawing room window and Miklos was just about to run ahead and tell his uncle what he had seen, when Forella heard voices and put her hand out to hold onto him.

"Wait a moment," she whispered.

She did not want to tell the Prince what had happened in the presence of somebody else.

Then, as she stood irresolutely, wondering how she could break the news to him of what had occurred, she heard him say angrily in a voice that she did not recognise,

"What are you saying, Jacques? And you have not yet explained why you are here."

He was speaking in French and, as Forella wondered who the stranger could be, a man answered,

"You have just two minutes, Kovác, to make up your mind what you will do, the choice is yours!"

"What the devil are you talking about?"

"I will make it very clear, Lucille and I came here together."

"Lucille is here?"

"Listen, you have no time to talk. She told the Nurse attending your wife that she had sprained her ankle and, while they were out of the room, somebody pushed that poor crazy creature out the window!"

"I have not the slightest idea what you are saying," the Prince exclaimed.

"The choice," Jacques went on as if he had not spoken, "is whether you swear that you will marry my sister or else be accused of murder! I am prepared to state that I saw you throw your wife out the window when there was nobody else in the room."

"I think you must be either mad or drunk!" the Prince said angrily. "My Head Groom was with me until one second before you came into the room."

"Your servant's evidence would not be admissible in a Court of Law when it comes to a case of murder," Jacques said scornfully. "So which is it to be, Kovác, marriage or a trial at the Old Bailey?"

It was then that Forella drew a deep breath and, taking Miklos by the hand, walked with him through the open window into the drawing room.

She had realised, while the Prince was talking to the Frenchman called 'Jacques', that the small boy did not understand French.

As they entered the drawing room together, she saw as she had expected that the man standing facing the Prince had a heavy black moustache and was the man she had seen at the window.

The Prince looked up as they appeared and before Forella could say anything, Miklos ran to his uncle's side.

"Uncle János," he cried, "I looked through the telescope and I saw a lady in white fall out of a window! I saw her!"

"You have just one minute more," the Frenchman said as if he wished to push aside the interruption.

"I also saw what happened," Forella said in French. "The 'Poor Lady' fell from the window, but she was pushed by a man who looked out to see where she had fallen."

She paused before she made a gesture with her hand towards the Frenchman and said,

"That was the man I saw!"

Jacques started and then he called out furiously,

"More servants' evidence? I doubt if it would carry any weight before a Judge and Jury."

"My name, *monsieur*, if you are interested," Forella said slowly in French, "is Forella Claye and my uncle is the Marquis of Claydon, who is the Lord-in-Waiting to Her Majesty Queen Victoria!"

She spoke clearly and positively and it was as if she watched the Frenchman crumble before her eyes.

He knew he was defeated and, although he wanted to bluster further, his eyes shifted and he seemed suddenly to grow smaller as the Prince said in a voice of authority,

"There is now one minute for you and Lucille to get out of this house and then out of the country! If you remain in the vicinity, you will be apprehended on a charge of murder and my guest who saw what happened will give evidence, which means that you will hang!"

Jacques opened his lips to speak and the Prince added in a voice of thunder,

"One minute!"

Then, as quickly as the 'Poor Lady' had fallen, Jacques ran from the room, slamming the door behind him.

Because she had been so tense and at the same time so afraid for the Prince, Forella felt as if the walls were moving round her and there was a darkness coming up from the floor.

But the Prince's arms supported her and he helped her to a sofa as Miklos was asking,

"Why did that man run away? I saw him in the window after the lady fell."

The Prince took his arms from Forella.

"Miklos," he said quietly, "I want you to do something for me."

"What is it, Uncle János?"

"I want you to go to the stables to look at the horses and take this lady with you."

"I would like to do that, Uncle János."

"You are to say nothing, do you understand, nothing of what you have seen or heard until you have talked to me about it. It is very important and I know you will do as I tell you."

"Yes, of course, Uncle János."

The Prince turned again to Forella.

"Are you all right?" he asked. "If so, I would like you to leave this room as quickly as you can."

"I-I am all – right," Forella replied in a whisper.

"You have saved me," the Prince said, "and now I want to save you and everybody else from a great deal of unpleasantness."

Forella rose to her feet.

The weakness had passed and she really did feel all right. It was because the Prince was near her, he had touched her and she loved him.

She put out her hand to Miklos.

"Come along," she urged. "I know you will enjoy seeing your uncle's horses."

The Prince walked to the door and opened it for them.

"Thank you," he said very softly as Forella passed him and the words were like a caress.

The hall was empty.

Then, as Forella and Miklos turned down the corridor which led them to the side door that was nearest to the stables, she saw Newman coming from the opposite direction.

He was moving very much more quickly than he usually did and she heard him saying breathlessly as he reached the Prince,

"I must ask Your Highness to come at once! There has been a terrible accident!"

*

Afterwards Forella found it difficult to remember exactly what had happened and in what order everything had taken place for it had all been so dramatic as to seem unreal.

It did not seem possible that the 'Poor Lady' was dead and that the Prince was now free.

Whilst she was in the stables with Miklos feeding the horses and pretending to listen while Thomas explained to the small boy how they had been bred and where they had come from, all she could think of was the Prince.

Perhaps after all his wife had suffered only from shock and had not been murdered as the Frenchman had intended.

She wondered vaguely just who he was and indeed who Lucille might be and also why the Prince should be blackmailed into marrying her.

Then she thought that it was only justice that, as he had saved her from being married to the Earl, so she had saved him from being forced into marrying somebody who must have conspired with her brother to murder the 'Poor Lady'.

It all seemed so complicated and so horrible and yet she could not help a little flicker of irrepressible happiness that, if the 'Poor Lady' was dead, the Prince was now a free man.

'Even if he does not – want me,' she thought, 'since I love him – I want his – happiness.'

Thomas lifted Miklos onto the back of one of the magnificent stallions.

"I want to ride this horse," Miklos said. "Do you think Uncle János will let me?"

"You will have to ask His Highness yourself," Thomas answered.

"There is no time today," Miklos said, "because Mama is waiting at The Castle to take me to a crammer."

"Perhaps next holidays," Thomas suggested with a smile.

"Yes, of course, next holidays," Miklos agreed.

Forella was wondering where she would be when the holidays came round and, if she would be in Hungary, from where Miklos had just come.

Her mind seemed to be going round and round in many circles and she kept seeing the outstretched arms of the 'Poor Lady' as she tried to find something to hold onto as Jacques pushed her from the window.

Now that she could think about it clearly, she knew that the Prince in telling him to get out of the house and out of the country was not seeking to save him from the consequences of his crime, but to avoid the scandal and publicity that would ensue from a murder trial.

It was not only something that he would shrink from and dislike above everything, but so many other people would suffer, like the Princess, the Doctor, Thomas and herself.

If the Police were brought in and it was a question of a trial, they would all be expected to give evidence and their anonymity would be swept away.

'Then Uncle George would know where I was without having to look for me,' Forella thought in horror.

She realised that last night when she had seen Jacques looking, as she thought, at her window, he had actually been looking up at the window where the 'Poor Lady' slept.

Now she was certain that he had been trying to find out for the last few days, when he had been snooping about and questioning the servants, how the household was organised.

He would have learnt that while one Nurse was having her luncheon, the other would be on duty alone. That was why Lucille, whoever she might be, had asked her to attend to her sprained ankle.

Jacques had thus made sure that there was nobody with the 'Poor Lady' when he entered the room and she was feeding her doves.

Watching her as he must have done, he would have become aware that the doves were greedy for anything she could give them and it had been easy for him, because she was small, to tip her out the window as Forella and Miklos had seen him do.

'It was a chance in a million,' Forella thought, 'that we should have been watching through Miklos's telescopes.'

And yet, perhaps it was a Power greater than chance that ensured that the Prince should not be accused of a really wicked deed that he would never in the nobility of his heart have contemplated.

It was as if her prayers had all been answered by God directly and, as she had prayed for his happiness, God had listened and had come to the rescue of them both.

"If only – that could be – true," Forella whispered to herself and was afraid that perhaps she was being far too optimistic.

Then, when they had just finished inspecting the horses, one of the footmen came to the stables to say that His Highness wished them to return to the house where he was waiting for them in the drawing room.

Nervous and afraid that something had happened that she did not anticipate, Forella was very pale as they went into the room.

The Prince was standing with his back to the fireplace, and, as they came in, he said,

"Miklos, I want you to go up the stairs and meet a relative of yours, the Princess Maria Dabás, who I told you about when we were coming here."

"I want to see her, Uncle János," Miklos said. "I have read about Imbe Dabás and how he was executed."

"Do not speak to her of that," the Prince warned, "but she is very eager to meet you and hurry because we must soon go back to The Castle. You will find that Newman is waiting at the bottom of the stairs to show you the way to the Princess."

Miklos left the drawing room and, as soon as he had gone, the Prince held out his hands to Forella.

"Listen, my darling," he started, "because there will be a great deal to do here, although I know that Dr. Bouvais will make things as easy as possible, I want you to leave immediately for a house I own on the way to Southampton."

Forella looked at him in perplexity and he went on,

"I will join you there later, but I want you to be brave enough to drive there alone and wait for me. Will you do that?"

"You know I will do – anything you – tell me to do," Forella answered, "but I don't – understand."

"I will explain everything," the Prince said, "but it is important that you should not be seen here now because you were brave enough to reveal your real name and also because an accident and a funeral will create huge gossip at least locally."

"I will – wait for – you."

The Prince raised her hand and kissed it.

"Thank you, my lovely one," he said softly. "Now go and get ready while I explain to the Princess what has occurred. The carriage will be waiting and I will delay everything else until you are gone."

"Thank you – *thank you*," Forella murmured.

He kissed her hand again and she went from the room and up the stairs to her bedroom.

She was not surprised to find that Mrs. Newman was already there.

"His Highness says you have to leave at once, my Lady," she said, "and that's very sad, coming on top of the bad news we've had already."

"I am so sorry for the 'Poor Lady'," Forella said quietly.

"We just have to believe that God knows best," Mrs. Newman sighed.

"That is what I have thought too," Forella agreed, thinking of how her prayers had been answered.

She changed hurriedly into her travelling clothes and ate a light meal that was brought up to her on a tray.

She found, when she went to say 'goodbye' to the Princess, that the Prince had already left The Manor to take Miklos to The Castle and then to visit the Chief Constable and explain to him that there had been an accident.

"If you ask me," the Princess said, "it is a merciful release, not only for Gisella but also, of course, for dear János, although it is certainly not the right thing to say at the moment."

"No – of course not," Forella murmured.

"I think we are all feeling apprehensive in case it gets into the newspapers," the Princess went on in a low voice.

"If they report who we are and ask why we are here, anything might happen."

"I am sure that the Prince will make certain that there is no scandal," Forella answered.

"Why should there be?" the Princess asked. "It was an accident and, although I believe that the poor Nurses are blaming themselves for leaving her alone, nobody except a complete hypocrite would pretend it was a tragedy."

"I must go – Your Highness."

"János told me he was sending you away," the Princess said. "I have loved having you here and the only thing I regret is that you have not told me your secret, which I think is very unkind of you, considering that you know mine!"

"I will tell you everything the next time we meet," Forella promised her and the Princess laughed.

"I have a feeling, although perhaps I am being clairvoyant, that that may be sooner than seems possible and perhaps your circumstances will be different from what they are at the moment."

Forella did not answer.

She saw that the Princess's eyes were bright with curiosity as she bent down and kissed her cheek.

"I promise that if I can," she said, "And I will write and tell you everything you want to know."

"Then make it soon," the Princess answered, "otherwise I shall die of sheer curiosity."

Forella laughed.

Then she ran downstairs to find a closed carriage waiting for her outside the door and her trunks with all her pretty new gowns in them stacked up behind.

She noted that the coachman was driving four very fine horses and, as they set off, she realised that the carriage that she was travelling in was very light.

She knew that they would not take very long to complete the journey and it would be a comfortable one.

It was a strange feeling indeed, setting off into the unknown, but because the Prince had arranged it she was not frightened but merely excited.

It was growing late in the afternoon when the horses turned in at the drive at the end of which was an attractive house of about the same size as The Manor. But it was of red brick and proclaimed by its windows and porticoed door that it had been built in the time of Queen Anne. .

There were servants waiting to greet her and Forella realised that a groom must have gone ahead to announce her arrival.

The butler, a younger man than Newman, but with the same air of consideration and efficiency, said,

"Welcome, my Lady."

This told Forella that she was still to use her mother's family name and, as she looked round the impressive marble hall, she exclaimed,

"What a lovely house this is!"

"His Highness bought it, my Lady, at the same time as he built his yacht, which he keeps at Southampton. It breaks the journey at exactly the right distance for the horses."

The butler smiled as he went on,

"His Highness, I'm ever so glad to say, does not care for those new-fangled, noisy and dangerous trains as a means of conveyance."

"Horses are much nicer," Forella replied.

"That's what I thinks, my Lady," the butler answered, "and you'll find some extra fine horseflesh in the stables, although I'm sure His Highness'll show them to you himself."

Because the Prince was coming to join her, even though as he had said it might be late, Forella went upstairs as if in a dream, knowing that, because she was waiting for him, time would pass slowly.

But the time was endowed with a special magic because he was really coming to her.

The elderly maid waiting on her suggested that she rest after her journey and actually, because all the events of the day had been so exhausting, Forella slept.

When she awoke it was to find that it was very much later than she had expected.

She had a bath and when she had dressed in one of the lovely gowns that the Prince had sent to her from London, she went down the stairs, expecting to dine alone.

However, when she reached the hall, the butler said,

"A groom has just arrived, my Lady, to say that His Highness is now on his way and, as I reckon he'll be with us in perhaps an hour's time, I thought you might prefer to wait dinner until His Highness arrives."

"Yes – of course," Forella agreed at once.

She went into the drawing room, which was a large room with a high ceiling and was furnished in the luxurious manner that was characteristic of all the Prince's possessions.

Flowers scented the air and the curtains had not been drawn as they looked out over a garden filled with roses and syringa.

'It is enchanted!' Forella thought.

She felt as if her heart was beating like the tick of the clock and repeating as it did so the Prince's name over and over again.

*

It was a little over an hour later when the door opened.

She was expecting him to appear in his riding clothes in which he must have travelled very swiftly.

Instead he must have reached the house without her being aware of it for he was in full evening dress.

He looked so magnificent and handsome that she gave a cry of delight not only because he was there but also because of his appearance.

The door closed behind him and, without thinking, conscious only of her joy, Forella ran towards him.

When she reached him, she would have checked herself, but his arms went round her and he held her close, and she could feel his heart beating against hers.

"My darling, my sweet," he said very softly. "I am sorry to have been so long."

"Is – everything – all right?"

She could barely say the words and it did not sound at all like her own voice asking the question.

"Everything," he said. "Come and sit down, and we will talk about it."

He took his arms from her and, because she knew that he expected it of her, she walked towards the sofa.

As she sat down, the door opened and servants came in with champagne, which they poured into crystal glasses that were engraved with the Prince's insignia.

"Dinner'll be ready in a few minutes, Your Highness," the butler said as he left the room.

"You must be hungry," the Prince said. "I did not expect you to wait for me."

He was speaking conventionally and yet what he said was unimportant.

What mattered was the look in his eyes, the deep note in his voice and the fact that he was so near to her that Forella was trembling with a wild excitement that made her feel as if she was floating on air.

What she ate and drank in the dining room and what they said to each other was later impossible to remember.

All she knew was that it seemed as if the angels were singing overhead and their music was a love song that united them as closely as if they were touching each other.

When they returned to the drawing room and now that the curtains were drawn and the candles lit in the chandeliers, the Prince said,

"We have so much to tell each other, but all I really want to say is how beautiful you are and how much you mean to me."

"Is — that true?"

"I think you know without any words how much I love you," the Prince said, "and my Hungarian instinct tells me, although you have never said so, that what you feel for me is the beginning of love."

"I do – love you wildly!" Forella admitted. "But I never – thought that I would be able – to tell you so."

"We should have trusted Fate, or perhaps God, who was looking after us,"

He gave a deep sigh before he went on,

"When I knew that I must send you away, I felt as if I was cutting my heart out of my body, but it was something essential that I had to do."

"Where – will you – send me now?" Forella asked.

She knew that it was a question that had been at the back of her mind all day.

The Prince smiled and it was as if the whole room was lit with a blazing light.

"I am sending you nowhere, my precious one," he replied. "I am taking you to Hungary after we are married."

"M-married?"

Forella found it hard to say the word and yet it had been spoken.

"It will not be the marriage that perhaps you had dreamt of with bridesmaids and a huge Reception," the Prince answered. "Because we have to be very secretive, I have arranged that we shall be married tomorrow morning in the little Church here in the village before we join my yacht at Southampton and start on our honeymoon."

Forella clasped her hands together.

"I-I cannot believe – what you are – saying."

"That is, of course," the Prince said, "if you are willing to marry me."

He paused to say quietly,

"I think, my darling, that we both know that a force, a Power stronger than ourselves, has joined us together and it would be impossible for us to live without each other."

"That is – true, but I did not – think that you would – marry me."

"You are what I have been looking for all my life," he said, "and whatever anybody else may think, I have no intention, having found you of ever losing you."

"That – is what I – wanted you to say," she answered. "But please – you are quite certain that I am the – right person, the right sort of wife – and I shall not fail you?"

The Prince gave a laugh that was one of sheer happiness.

"I am quite, quite certain," he then said. "It is going to take a very long time, perhaps an Eternity, to convince you of how much I love you and how certain I am that you are the wife who was born just for me and that we can never lose each other again, never!"

The way he spoke was very moving.

Then gently he put his arms around Forella and drew her close to him.

He looked down at her for a long moment.

"How can you be so perfect, so exquisite," he asked, "that I find it hard even when I am touching you to believe that you are real?"

He did not wait for her to reply.

His lips came down on hers and she knew at the touch of them that this was what she had been longing for and aching for ever since she had realised that she loved him.

At first his mouth was very gentle, then, as he felt her whole body melting into his and her lips surrendered themselves so completely to him, his kiss became more insistent, more demanding and very much more possessive.

He held her closer and still closer until she felt a wild rapture seep through her.

It moved from her breast into her throat and from her throat into her lips, where the fire that seemed to come from the Prince ignited a fire within her too.

It was so ecstatic that she could hardly believe it was actually happening.

Then, as he kissed her and went on kissing her, she could no longer think.

She could only feel that he had carried her up into a Heaven where they were alone and they touched the Divine.

When at last the Prince raised his head, Forella managed to say incoherently,

"I – love – you! *I love – you!* Can this – really be – happening to us? I think I must be – dreaming!"

"Then I am dreaming too," the Prince said, "but our dreams have come true. I have found you and, my precious, I have been so desperately afraid, because I was not free to ask you to be my wife that I would lose you."

She knew by the way he spoke that it had been a very real fear for him.

She thought how she had felt in despair that there were so many beautiful women in his life that he would have no time for her.

Then she knew that their love was different from anything they might feel or think about other people and, as the Prince had said, they were one person.

He was looking into her eyes and. as if he knew what she was thinking, he said,

"My darling, my bride, my heart, my soul and without exception, the most perfect rider I have ever seen!"

Because it was so far from what she had expected him to say, Forella gave a gurgling little laugh.

"Am I really a – good rider?" she asked.

"Of course," he replied, "and we will ride together on horses that I believe are the best in the world and certainly the most spirited and very very wild."

Forella drew in her breath as she added,

"It all sounds so wonderful – but you know the only thing that really – matters is that – you will be there with me. I did not want to go to Hungary when you said you would – send me there, because it meant leaving you behind."

"That is something you will never do in the future," the Prince said. "Oh, my darling, I never knew I could find such happiness so unexpectedly after so many years of feeling alone even in the midst of a crowd."

Because she suddenly felt protective towards him, Forella reached up to touch his cheek with her hand.

"I will never – let you be alone again," she vowed, "and I want – more than anything – else in the world – to give you a son."

The Prince looked at her as if he could hardly believe what she had just said.

Then without replying he kissed her passionately, demandingly and rather differently.

She knew that she had excited him and she had offered him what he longed for and she could fill his life as no other woman had ever been able to do.

"I love you – I – *love you*!" she said, because there were no other words to express her feelings.

"And I adore you," the Prince said. "Tomorrow, my darling, you will be mine and there will be no more problems and no more unhappiness."

He paused and added,

"And no more lonely nights of lying awake and thinking about you, knowing that there was no possible way I could make you mine and all your sublime help has come from the heart."

The passion in his voice was very moving and, as he felt a little tremor go through her, he said,

"I have so much to teach you, my precious love, so much to awaken in your heart, your mind and your beautiful body, which is very Hungarian."

Forella knew what he meant and gave a little laugh of sheer happiness.

Then he was kissing her again and it was impossible to think of anything except that nothing mattered in the future except that he should be with her.

She was his, as he was hers, for all Eternity.

Now that they were together, no one could divide them or spoil their love, which filled the whole world and had been given to them directly by God.